MW00477551

CHRISTMAS IN PARADISE

PARADISE SERIES
BOOK 13

DEBORAH BROWN

CHRISTMAS IN PARADISE
All Rights Reserved
Copyright © 2017 Deborah Brown

ISBN-13: 978-0-9984404-3-9

Cover: Natasha Brown

PRINTED IN THE UNITED STATES OF AMERICA

CHRISTMAS IN PARADISE

Chapter One

"Jingle bells, jingle bells…" Santa encouraged the well-dressed older women lined up, ready to sit in his lap, to sing off-key at the top of their lungs. It was clear that it wasn't shopping that brought the women to the only outdoor mall in Tarpon Cove, the lot of them decked out in huge smiles, blowing kisses. A couple of them I recognized as "friends" of Crum's.

Santa waved his arms, encouraging their raucous behavior. At the end of the song, he clapped and bowed, which left the women giggling like schoolgirls.

The ill-fitting suit in the corner, who had mall management written all over him, stomped over, steam practically rising from his head.

Whatever tirade he was about to unleash came to an abrupt halt when the twenty-five-foot Christmas tree rocked side to side, toppling over and partially covering Santa's gingerbread house, which the mall had built for the big man's "family" and used for processing the pictures of the children who sat on Santa's lap. Large ornaments crashed to the ground, sending shards of glass flying.

From where I was standing, I could see that Mrs. Claus had awoken from her drunken stupor and stumbled into the tree… and by whatever miracle escaped going down with it. She covered her dismay at the crunching under her feet with a giggle and lurched over to Santa's throne, making herself comfortable and hiking up her skirt, mumbling, "Damn dress."

A few of the women in line screamed, jumping back. Two of them attempted to squeeze under the velvet rope. To jump into Santa's arms? That turned out to be a bad idea – one's bouffant got stuck on the stand and brought the barricade tumbling down on their backs. They lay in a heap, arguing over whose fault it was that they were sprawled on the ground.

The handful of children in line started crying. Too much adult drama.

"Fabiana Merceau, get back over here," I hissed at my partner, who was trying to slink off into a shoe store located temptingly close. If I was going to have a headache, then so was she. That's what best friends did – they shared.

Fab stomped over to my side, arms crossed. "Madison Westin," she mimicked. "Crum had the nerve to suggest that I be one of Santa's elves. The costume is threadbare, ugly, and it smells. And even if it were brand new, I wouldn't do it." She added, "No way!"

It took everything I had not to burst out laughing. We had been drinking eggnog lattes at our favorite bakery when I got a frantic call from Santa.

"Everything's gone south on me," Crum, the shopping center's newest Santa, had huffed. "The missus passed out. One elf didn't show. I really need your help. Get over here as quick as you can."

I'd managed to hold back a loud snort, but just barely. "What exactly do you want me to do?" I asked before realizing he'd hung up.

I hadn't bothered to fill Fab in on what was happening, being deliberately vague because I knew I wouldn't stand a chance of her setting one of her designer shoes into the middle of this mess if she knew about it in advance, especially if she found out it had anything to do with Crum. At least, not without intense blackmail.

Professor Crum resided at The Cottages, some beachfront property I owned. He loved women and drama and always had some unsuitable moneymaking scheme up his sleeve. I'd almost laughed when he told me he'd gotten the Santa job, thinking uncharitably that no one else must have applied.

Fab and I had arrived just in time to snag a good vantage point where we could see the drama unfold and overhear every word.

The mall suit jerked Crum by the arm, trying to drag him off to one side, but Santa dug in his boots, slowing their progress. "I let you choose your own *helpers,* and what a disaster that's turned out to be." The man's anger vibrated through his body. "The only reason you're not fired on the spot is that I can't get a replacement here today. Now you listen to me – if you need this job as much as you say you do, get your act together and now."

The old "poor mouth" routine. Crum demonstrated all the eccentricities of a bag person but was far from one. He was a retired college professor with a healthy pension.

"I'll take care of everything," Crum reassured the man. He turned, rolling his eyes, caught sight of me, and almost tripped over his feet getting to me before I could duck out.

I'd put money on his idea of taking care of the problem being throwing a hissy fit or walking off the job in a huff. The only thing stopping him was all the people around, who would laugh about it for the next decade.

The man stopped in front of me, out of breath, his agitation at an all-time high. "Get Miss January out of here," Crum said to me in a mini-panic. "Then hurry back." He ran his eyes over me. "You'll fit in the dress." At my puzzled expression, he said, "Think of the children." He glared at Fab, who'd started laughing. "Fab doesn't give a damn about the kiddies and their happiness. Besides, she's too fat for the dress."

As funny as I thought that was, I bit back my laughter. I knew my friend didn't have an ounce of fat on her and was in kick-butt shape.

Spinning around, I grabbed her wrist and cautioned, "Do not shoot him." When Fab's glare calmed to a simmer, I dropped her hand and turned back to Crum. "If you value your body parts in their current location, I suggest you curtail your comments."

The tops of his cheeks, which showed above the bedraggled beard, turned bright red. He scuffed the ground with the toe of his boot, mumbling incoherently.

What the man wanted finally sank in. "You expect me to be Mrs. Claus?" Time for Plan B. I had no intention of being sucked in by his sentimental drivel. "I don't need your high IQ to figure out that, since this entire area is a mess, you'll be closing the gingerbread house for the day. Unless management moves your location, which is probably not doable. But either way, they need to get everything cleaned up. I suggest that you get your ho-ho-ho on and go over and schmooze the kids, making this an experience to remember as opposed to a disaster." Being a fan of the big man myself – the traditional version anyway – I frowned at the thought of the kids not having fun. "Not even one glance at your fan club," I scolded. "Those hussies need to go shopping, which will please the management."

My very first job had been as a Santa's helper. He'd been a drunken lech. Every day, me and Mrs. Claus laughed at his jokes, even though I didn't understand most of them. I never confided in Mother, instinctively knowing that the job would come to an abrupt end if I did.

The mall manager—whose nametag read Jared Greg—was back, a maintenance man by his side. "You're fired." He glared at Crum. "We're closing Santa's village."

"Wait," I interjected. "This situation is salvageable. When are you planning to reopen?"

"Who are you?" Jared snapped.

"A friend." I nodded in Crum's direction.

"That's not much of a reference."

"I can get replacements here so you can re-open this afternoon. That's if you do your part and get this cleaned or moved – whatever. You might want to rethink firing Santa, though. Him, I can't replace, and it was his idea to salvage the experience for the children." I tried to shove Crum forward, but he once again dug in his worn boots, trimmed in fur that looked suspiciously like cotton balls glued together.

I'd heard he had to supply his own shoes, and from a brief glance, it appeared they were a major score from a dumpster. The man loved his unusual hobby, told me once that dumpster diving calmed his nerves after a stressful day. It would have been a good story if I hadn't known he made his rounds in the early morning hours on trash day.

Crum stepped forward and spoke to the manager, selling my idea with enthusiasm, excitement in his voice, his arms waving. He had storytelling down to an art.

Jared clapped him on the shoulder. "You get these women to go shopping, spend some money, and you're rehired." He practically salivated at visions of dollar signs. "Get your butt over there, take pictures with the children, and get them thinking about sugar plums and fairies. You better not mention coal again, no matter what you think of the kid."

"Can't you ever mind your own business?" Fab asked from behind me.

I turned and mouthed, "Holiday spirit."

"Forgot who I was talking to for a minute," Fab said with melodrama. "In case you thought of asking, I'm not taking on extra work at this time."

I fished my phone out of my pocket and walked away, knowing that would annoy her. "Need your help," I said when my property manager, Mac, answered the phone. I went on to tell her the events of the morning.

Mac Lane managed The Cottages. I'd hired her to corral the guests and long-term tenants and keep them out of trouble. To say she'd worked out well was an understatement. Another of her great attributes was she never said no.

"I wondered how long Crum would last," Mac said. "Should have tried to hustle up a few side bets. Probably wouldn't have gotten any takers."

"I need a Mrs. Claus and an elf. No drunks… or only the ones that can hold off until they get off work." The Cove being a small touristy town, the shops closed at six unless there was a big event. "Bonus in it for you if I can make this your problem and not mine."

"I suppose you want me to start now, once again without the notice a reasonable person gives?" Mac sniffed.

"If you weren't such a superstar at problem-handling, you wouldn't be my first call."

"Flattery. Love it." Mac laughed. "I'll be the missus until I can get a replacement, and I'll bring Joseph along with me. He's not ideal, but I can boss him around easy enough."

I winced at the thought of Joseph being involved. "Maybe... look for someone to replace him also. I'll make it clear to Crum that you're top dog—you call the shots, and he better damn well listen."

"I'm going to enjoy every minute of this job." A smile was evident in her voice. "What about Miss January?"

"Since Fab probably won't let her sit in the SUV, we'll tie her to the roof and bring her home."

Both Miss January and Joseph were tenants inherited with the property. Of the two, Joseph managed to stay sober at least half the day while Miss January could only manage a few hours.

Fab banged her head on my shoulder. When I walked off, she'd followed and gotten close enough to listen to both sides of the conversation without me having to use the speaker. I'd say it was shocking behavior, but it wasn't. The woman couldn't stand to be left out of anything, and it never mattered that she said she wasn't the least bit interested.

"I'll be there in a half-hour, assuming Joseph is dressed."

I flinched, not wanting that image to take hold. I put my phone away, and me and my shadow headed straight over to Crum. "Mac's got this handled. Don't upset her in any way," I told him, adding a finger jab. "Just a reminder: you owe me big… huge, in fact."

"I knew if I called you, you'd help. Anyone else would hang up on me." Crum had mustered up a pitiful tone. "You're the best friend I've ever had. My only one, really."

I felt a poke in my back. Not wanting to ruin this greeting card moment, I said, "Hmm…" Doing my best to make it sound like an appropriate response. I waved him off to the children, who were anxiously awaiting his return. Now that the female hangers-on had been cleared out, the line was down to a manageable dozen.

"Ready?" I asked Fab.

"Finally. I have a great idea."

Probably not, judging by the cagey look on her face, but I didn't say anything.

"We'll send Miss January home in a cab and be there to pick her up."

"Maybe."

Fab grumbled about our next task until I couldn't take it anymore and gave her one of Mother's "you better behave" stares. We found Miss January passed out in the last place we'd seen her, no one apparently wanting to wake the snoring woman. I came close to threatening Fab with bodily harm before she finally relented and we each took an arm and hauled the woman up and off Santa's throne, guiding her down a long hallway to the dressing room. There, Fab sliced her finger through the air, letting me know she wasn't having any part of the next stage of the plan.

I helped Miss January out of her costume, hanging the skirt, blouse, and jacket up for Mac to wear. The tag read, "one size fits all," but without the belt, the dress would've swallowed up the woman. On Mac, it would create a totally different look—the next Mrs. Claus would be all womanly curves.

I'm not sure who'd thought it was a good idea to talk Miss January into doing this gig. Being a betting woman, my dollar was on Crum having no other options and running out of time. The diminutive grey-haired woman drank and smoked from the moment her head rolled off the pillow. How she managed to control her nicotine habit, sometimes for hours at a time, had amazed me. Then one day, I found nicotine gum in her pocket. She'd opened one eye and mumbled, "Almost choked," and pointed at the package. I threw it away and fished through her pockets, getting rid of the rest.

Getting her dressed was a lot easier, only requiring that I slide her muumuu over her head and shove her feet into a pair of slippers. At that point, I needed Fab's help to get her out of the building and into the car. Without her help, Miss January and I would both end up in a heap in the middle of the parking lot. I snapped my fingers in frustration, pointing for Fab to once again grab an arm.

On the way out, I grabbed a trash bag off a janitor's cart, fairly sure the woman wouldn't get sick but just covering my bases.

Fab eyed the bag and snapped, "What if she misses the bag?"

"I'll call the crime scene cleaner guy. He can get dead smell out of a house; sick smell out of a car ought to be easy-peasy." I ignored her death stare. "We'll put the seats down, shove her in the back, and I'll sit with her. The rubber mats back there are expendable." If you didn't know how our relationship worked, you'd think my SUV belonged to Fab, as I rarely got to drive it.

I'd finally gotten my Hummer back after its long stay at the auto body shop. Most of my relatives had noticed its disappearance from the driveway and suggested that, had I used the family business for the repairs, I'd have gotten it back long ago. But then everyone would know I'd lied when I passed off the "minor damage" as the result of a little fender bender, minimizing the details of the incident that had left the SUV totaled and me using the insurance check to get it fixed. Every time I walked by it, I scrutinized it for damage and couldn't find any. It had even passed Fab's white-glove inspection.

It took both Fab and I to heave Miss January into the back. She drifted in and out of her stupor, barely noticing her change in surroundings. I climbed in next to her, trash bag in hand.

For once, Fab didn't drive like a crazy woman, dodging and weaving in traffic. She still managed to make it to The Cottages in record time, and pulled into the driveway of the U-shaped ten-unit beachfront property with no additional drama.

I pushed open the back door and grabbed hold of Miss January's legs, pulling her to the edge, sitting her up, and placing her feet on the ground. The door of her cottage slammed opened. Her boyfriend stood on the top step, staring, as though trying to figure out was happening. What was his name again? I was getting as bad as Fab. In my defense, he kept a low profile.

They were an unlikely couple, looking like

grandmother and grandson when they were actually close to the same age. Miss January was a good example of hard living taking its toll.

"What happened?" he asked, concern in his voice.

"Drunk on the job. She got fired," I said.

"I knew it was bad idea, but she was so excited." He scooped her up and carried her into the cottage, kicking the door closed.

"Thank you to you too," I yelled after him and flounced back to the car.

"I..." Fab said as she slid behind the wheel, then appeared stuck as to what to say next.

I waved my hand. "I'm mostly certain that whatever it is that is about to come out of your mouth isn't the least bit holiday-ish, and I won't stand for it." I gave her a demented stare, trying to cross my eyes, which I wasn't very good at. Probably a good thing.

I flipped on the radio. Jingle Bells blared out of the speakers, and we both laughed.

Chapter Two

Halfway home, Fab's phone rang. She glanced at the screen. "You answer it."

"Nope." I flipped open the mirror on the visor, turning my head from side to side. I thought my red curls looked tame, considering the humidity. I didn't bother to compare with my friend's almost waist-length hair, never a brown strand out of place.

The phone stopped ringing. Fab expressed her displeasure by making a noise I hadn't heard before. "What are you doing?" she snapped.

"Checking to see if I have 'stupid' tattooed on my forehead. Go ahead and look at me with a straight face and tell me that wasn't a problem of some sort. Disgruntled client, perhaps—one that's madder than one of those black bees with the red polka dots."

"'Madder than hell' would have been quicker."

"We don't use those kinds of words during the holiday season."

"You're taking this 'cheery' business way too far." Fab's blue eyes burned into me.

"It's only going to get worse," I assured her. "So get ready."

Her phone started ringing again. "Answer it."

This time I did. "Deck the halls…" I started singing without looking at the screen.

A male voice laughed. "I know this isn't Fab."

I pulled the phone from my ear and glanced at the screen. "Just as I suspected. Hi Raul, it's me, Madison."

Raul and Dickie owned the Tropical Slumber Funeral Home. Raul ran the business side, Dickie the final preparations, which he'd informed me once was an art and needed to be executed with care.

"We have an emergency. Do the two of you have time to come by as soon as possible?"

"Fab's not feeling well—" I started.

"I'm better now," Fab yelled. "We're on our way." She jerked the wheel, making a sudden turn, a nearby driver expressing their annoyance by laying on the horn. She flew down Main Street past some of our favorite stores.

"We'll be there in less than five," I said, successfully keeping the groan out of my voice.

"You didn't even ask what he wanted," Fab said in exasperation.

"I didn't want to know, and if you did, you should've taken the call." I turned to look out the passenger window, thinking about jumping out at the next signal. "Since he runs a funeral home, my guess is it has something to do with dead people. Maybe they 'misplaced' another body or one woke up from the afterlife *again*. I don't know why I let you drag me into these things—he's *your* friend."

"I can't help it if people like me."

I couldn't help myself—I laughed. Most people were afraid of the daunting Frenchwoman. A couple of inches short of six feet in the four-inch stilettos she favored, the woman packed some scary along with her sidekick – her Walther.

"You've got one hour to solve whatever the problem is and get me back home. I have a contractor coming and don't want to be late." I'd just over-hyped my appointment, but I didn't care as long as it got me back to the house on time. "Or let me out now, and I'll walk." I was happy that she didn't pull over. Besides it being too far, I wasn't in the mood for a hike; it was hot outside.

"Contractor?" She pulled into the funeral home parking lot and parked alongside the red carpet—the official welcome mat that extended several feet out into the parking lot from the front door. Since there wasn't a hearse parked on it, I assumed services were done for the day.

I ignored her question, thinking the element of surprise was my best bet. Before she could question me further, I hopped out of the SUV. Twin Dobermans, Astro and Necco, bounded out the door, skidding to a stop at my feet.

"No sandwiches." I held out my hands, and they took a sniff. I scratched them behind the ears, and both seemed content.

Raul and Dickie stood in the doorway, Raul with an indulgent smile on his face, Dickie appearing tired. It surprised me when they came outside, closing the distance between us — that rarely happened, if ever. Usually, we sat inside. I'd have to poke my head inside later and check for leftover funeral food that I could share with the dogs. The little sandwiches were a favorite.

The funeral duo couldn't be more different looks-wise. Raul with a body builder physique, and Dickie was tall and thin, with a pasty pallor. They were loyal friends to me and Fab and would do anything for either of us – all we had to do was ask. When we had in the past, they'd delivered. I just didn't have the same fascination with all things dead as my bestie, who'd just slammed the driver's door and now stood next to me.

"We've been robbed," Dickie said.

Not again. I tried to follow the dramatic flourish of his hands, but they went wild.

"Someone stole our Christmas decorations," Raul said.

Fab and I turned to the large grassy lawn. *Sure enough.* We'd driven by a couple of nights ago to check out this year's design, and since then, the area had definitely been vandalized. The thieves had left the artificial tree — my guess due to the stakes that kept it from falling—but the train set, candy cane village, lights, even Santa and the other inflatables… gone.

"Any obvious suspects?" Fab asked, taking her phone out of the pocket of her black jeans and snapping pictures.

Raul shook his head. "When we woke up this morning and took the dogs for a walk, we couldn't believe our eyes when we saw that most everything was gone. The thief obviously didn't take care about preserving the condition of anything and even damaged some of the decorations that were left behind."

"We called the police. Deputy came out, took a report. Shocked me when he said it wasn't uncommon at this time of the year." Dickie sighed heavily. "After he left, Raul and I cleaned up the debris. We couldn't figure out why the reindeer were left behind until we found out the vandal had poked holes in them. They're completely unusable."

"Did the cops by any chance suggest a motive for these types of thefts?" I asked.

"There's money in used decorations, both high-end and cheap," Dickie said sadly. "They get resold online or at flea markets."

"Get this." Raul snorted. "Some of these thieves steal to decorate their own houses."

I couldn't picture decking out my house with stolen decorations, only to have someone compliment one and ask where I got a particular item. *Oh, I stole it from the funeral home.*

"Hopefully you took pictures of your display before you cleaned up." At his nod, I said, "Forward me copies and a list of the missing items, if you have one, and we'll check it out." I had little hope of recovering anything. It could come down to a case of: "That's my Santa. No, it's mine."

Fab hugged Raul. "Be prepared to have to replace the stuff on your own."

Dickie and I looked at each other awkwardly. Neither of us did touchy-feely, my emphasis being on the touch part, as in don't unless I initiate it.

"I know a couple of people that might be able to scare up a few items, as long as you don't mind gently used," I said. Old finds were a passion. I tended towards wrought iron and metal items but knew I could rustle up some yard decorations.

Growing bored, either Astro or Necco nudged my hand, a ball in his mouth. Wrestling it from his mouth, I threw it. Both dogs took off in a chase. One dog beat out the other, which had me laughing. They snagged the ball back and forth as they made their way back for me to throw it again.

"We've got another appointment," Fab said. "I'll keep you updated."

I threw the ball once more and followed Fab back to the car.

As Fab pulled back out onto the street, I asked, "You're the PI, what's the plan?"

"As backup, that's your job."

"We could hit the yard sales this weekend, snap up anything we find. Replace the inflatable Snow family as a gift, offer our condolences, and close the case."

She stared, unamused. "You need more caffeine?"

"No, this is my way of telling you there's no happy ending here."

Chapter Three

Fab blew into the driveway, sliding in next to her pristine black Porsche 911. There were times she came within a hair's breadth, and I'd grit my teeth, hoping not to hear the unmistakable scraping sound of sideswiping vehicles.

I had inherited the white two-story Key West-style house from my aunt and put my mark on the property inside and out. I always had a potential project floating around in my thoughts, which was what had brought me home early today.

As soon as we turned the corner, I noticed our boyfriends' cars parked across the street in the neighbor's driveway. At their insistence, we used it for parking whenever they weren't in town for the occasional weekend getaway.

"Let's hope one or both of the guys has an apron on with plans to feed us," I said.

"There's always take-out."

I turned up my nose. "We should surprise them and cook one night."

"That's a terrible idea." Fab got out, slamming the door, and headed to the house.

I was about to follow when a pickup blocked

the driveway. I changed course and walked over.

Fab skidded to a stop and called, "You need help?"

"This is my appointment." I waved her away and waited until the door closed behind her.

Jake Lawler, an electrical contractor who specialized in hanging outdoor lights this time of year, climbed out of his truck. In his fifties and friendly, the man could start a conversation with anyone. I'd met him via a referral from a customer at Jake's, a tropical dive bar I owned.

"Good news," he said. "My guys just finished up your property on the Overseas Highway this morning. Looks good. Tested everything myself; you shouldn't have any problems. Next will be The Cottages. Per your request, we'll try not to make it too gaudy."

Before I could answer, the front door banged open. Both of us turned as my boyfriend, Creole, came out of the house, pulling a t-shirt over his head, not giving me a second to ogle his muscular chest before he stalked across the driveway to where we stood.

"Creole" was his undercover moniker, which we all used despite the fact that he was currently on leave from the Miami police department. If we ever started calling him by his real name, no one would know who we were talking about.

"Who are you?" Creole demanded in a deep, bossy baritone. He grabbed my arm, pulling me to his side.

I sighed. "Whatever Fab told you was probably highly exaggerated, or possibly an outright lie." I made the introductions.

Didier, Fab's boyfriend, stuck his head out the door, yelled, "Hey Jake," and waved. The chilly air that had engulfed the three of us despite the ninety-degree heat warmed considerably at that acknowledgement.

I stepped in front of Creole and stared up into his face, demanding his full attention. "This is a surprise. You can go back and finish your... swim?" I glanced down at his bathing trunks and did a slow sweep up to his dark hair, sticking on end.

"I don't like surprises," he said, his tone not as deep as before.

"Me neither. That's one of the reasons we're perfect for one another."

Jake tried to disguise a laugh, but we both heard him.

Creole leaned forward and whispered, "I'll be watching out the window."

"Later," I said, full of promise.

Once the door closed, I reached into my purse, retrieving an envelope and handing it to Jake. "This is what I want. My drawings are crude, but you'll get the idea. The gate code is at the bottom." I tossed a glance over my shoulder. "It's one assigned only to your guys. Anyone asks any questions, you don't know anything." I zipped my lips. "Refer all nosiness to me."

"You've got to be the most organized client I've got, and I'm liking it a lot." He ripped open the envelope and took out the sheet of paper, reading my notes. He flipped it over, chuckling at the drawings.

"I want you to test the code, make sure it works okay." Taking the lead to the side gate, I paused briefly in front of the kitchen garden window and waved.

To my relief, the gate opened without a hitch. It was my first try at the guest-code thing. When Fab heard it was the latest technology, she didn't hesitate to have it installed on our security system. I'd reminded her to keep it simple for those not electronically minded, which as it turned out was just me.

Inside the gate, I led him down the path, and once in the backyard, did some finger-pointing, speaking in low tones about what I wanted where, all under the watchful eye of Fab, who glared from a chaise. She had to have broken the speed record for changing into her bathing suit.

"Turnaround on this is one to two days." He waved and left.

"I know what you're up to," Didier said to me, sitting down next to his girlfriend. The French duo were a made-for-each-other couple.

"Listen up, you three," I said as Creole appeared behind me. "You're going to get into the holiday spirit. No excuses. Don't think I won't whisper to Santa that you three should get coal." I gave brief thought to punctuating my words by stamping my foot, but that would only invite laughter. "I'm going to change." I turned to go inside, but Creole produced a sprig of mistletoe, holding it over my head and swooping in for a kiss, claiming my lips.

"You sure know how to make a guy look bad," Didier grumped.

"Catch." Creole tossed it to Didier, who caught it in one hand. "It's not a one-use-only deal." He scooped me off my feet and carried me through the French doors into the house.

We'd just finished the dinner Didier had prepared, his choice of food much to Fab's disgust – barbequed hamburgers with a platter of vegetables, every imaginable choice to pile on top. I inquired about french fries and got a blank stare.

The doorbell rang. Within a second, the ringing began again and continued non-stop.

"That's one of Fab's friends," I said.

"She has friends?" Creole asked, his mouth twitching in amusement.

"Me, and I'm accounted for." I smiled at her.

When it became clear no one was going to find out who was playing on the bell, Didier stood.

"There's a gun in the junk drawer," I said to his retreating back.

Didier returned with Kevin Cory in tow. The deputy sheriff was waved into a chair. Knowing his drinking habits, Didier got a soda out of the outside refrigerator and put it down in front of him.

"Sorry to interrupt," Kevin said. He was decked out in his uniform, which could only mean official business. That and the fact that he never came to my house for any other reason.

"Sure you are," Fab snarked.

"Good evening, officer." Creole nodded. "Before you get started, we all have alibis."

"I tend to forget how funny the bunch of you think you are," Kevin said dryly. "No arrest warrant." He held out his hands. "Looking for Crum. Thought you might make my job easy and tell me where to find him."

"You thought you'd find him here?" My tone of voice conveyed that he'd lost his mind.

"Eww." Fab followed up her declaration with a choking noise.

Kevin sat stoically. The guys laughed. I'd have to have a talk with them… let them know that laughter only encouraged Fab's outrageousness, and in truth, mine.

"You might want to start with where he lives," I said. "The same place you live. He doesn't have a bell," I said, expressing my disapproval at Kevin's antics. "If you don't get an answer after incessant knocking, check with Mac. If she doesn't know, then you're out of luck."

"What's he wanted for?" Creole asked. "I'm assuming that's the reason for the house call."

"Questioning in a bank robbery," Kevin told us in his official voice, so I knew it wasn't some weird prank.

"He wouldn't do that," I said adamantly. "You've got the wrong man." I didn't think it would be helpful to remind Kevin that it wouldn't be the first time he'd fingered the wrong person. I'm a good example of him doing that. "He doesn't need the money, and besides, he's got a job as a mall Santa."

"Santa." Kevin snorted.

"What makes you suspect him?" Creole asked.

"The suspect's been holding up banks in a Santa suit. The top part, anyway. On the bottom, he had on red bathing trunks."

Didier, the ex-fashion model turned real estate developer, winced at that description. He had on red swim trunks, but there was no confusing the intense, dark-haired, blue-eyed Frenchman for the white-haired, cantankerous man in question.

"If it were red tighty-whities or a skirt made from a bath towel, I'd say you have your man," I said. "Did your robber have on rubber boots or worn flip-flops?"

Kevin shook his head. "That wasn't in the police report."

"I'm telling you, it's not him," I defended Crum.

"Just missed Crum on the job—he doesn't

hang out there after hours," Kevin said. "So where's he now?"

"He's got a male friend or two; they like to cruise the cheap bars," I said.

"What Madison means is that he likes to get laid and finds a never-ending stream of eager, likeminded partners that way," Fab said, clearing up any confusion, not that Kevin could have any after living in close proximity to Crum.

Whatever Didier did, Fab squeaked, then glared at him. He was a stickler for appropriate talk, and the two of us broke that rule on a constant basis.

"Before you skip out the door, I've got a couple of questions. I'll trade another can of soda for the answers," I said.

"That might be construed as bribery." He flashed a smile, amused at himself.

"Okay then, no soda. We might be able to help you solve another case." I pointed at Fab and me.

"This ought to be good."

Creole and Didier were listening before, but now they leaned forward, waiting to hear what I wanted.

"Though you weren't the responding officer, I'm sure you've heard that the funeral home got their Christmas deco ripped off. Got any leads, by any chance?" I asked.

"No idea—didn't get assigned that one. My luck, when I get the call to go there, it will probably be about a dead body."

"There was that one time when the corpse woke up," I reminded him.

He frowned at me.

"Any chance Dickie and Raul will get their decorations back?"

Kevin shook his head. "Not unless they have them marked in some way, proving ownership. Stealing decorations is big this time of year. There's usually no arrest, except on the rare occasions where the thief is caught red-handed or gets drunk and brags. Mostly, it's just a matter of taking the report for insurance purposes." He looked at Fab and me. "I suppose they hired the two of you? I wouldn't put that on my PI resume, if I were you." He directed that at Fab.

"It's a freebie," I said. "You should be nice. One day, you'll croak—hopefully from old age—and you'll want a nice send-off, and what they'll remember is all the times you were less than cordial."

Whatever he was about to say, one look at Creole and he changed his mind.

His silence spurred me on. "Leave enough money for food and liquor in your will, and you'll have a huge turnout. People you never met will stumble up to the podium and mumble something nice."

Kevin stood, a look of pure disgust on his face. "I earned that second soda by having to listen to this." He crossed to the refrigerator and helped himself. "If you see Crum, tell him I want to talk to him. Remind him he can't hide forever. If he doesn't have anything to do with the robberies, it's in his best interest to clear himself as a suspect." He left without so much as a wave.

"That was fun," I said.

"Why is this the first Creole and I are hearing about this decoration heist?" Didier tried for a fierce look and failed.

"Any slain inflatables you two failed to mention?" Creole smirked.

"The reindeer. Wasn't it?" I turned to Fab for confirmation.

Fab shrugged. "Flip you for who breaks it to Raul and Dickie." She raised her eyebrow.

I produced an imaginary coin out of thin air, set it on the end of my thumb, and flipped it in the air. Forgetting to catch it, I declared, "You."

Chapter Four

Creole dropped a kiss on my forehead when he left at daylight to go for an early morning run with Didier. After that, they were headed down to the docks to check on some cleanup work in progress on a construction project Didier was managing. I rolled over and immediately went back to sleep until I was roused by a pounding on the bedroom door.

"What the…" I yelled, blinking sleep fog from my brain. I recognized the noise as, most likely, a tennis shoe being applied vigorously to the bottom panel of the door.

"Coffee's ready!" Fab yelled back, kicked the door again, and then silence.

"*Her* coffee is ready," I mumbled, heading to the shower. The thought of going downstairs disheveled, my hair sticking on end, had me smiling.

After a shower—during which I gave serious thought to using all the hot water, but I didn't, knowing Fab would be back if I didn't hurry—I rummaged through my closet, pulling on a black, knee-length skirt and sleeveless shirt and slipping into a pair of tennis shoes, not bothering with the laces. I stopped at the top of the staircase, and in an attempt to make as much noise as possible, I placed my hand gently on the railing, not wanting to disturb the greenery and ornaments I'd wrapped around it, and jumped down the stairs to the bottom. Every other step, I emitted a different animal noise, which I'd been told I never got right. At the bottom, I paused to enjoy the decorations in the living room and the tree in the corner, bursting with ornaments and strands of lights. It had been suggested that I overdid it, which I ignored.

I stopped in the entry, toed off my shoes, and kicked them into the tray by the door, then turned and skidded into the kitchen, throwing out my arms. "Bon-jury."

Other than rolling her eyes, Fab didn't respond to my antics. She pointed to a mug and my can of coffee mix. "One cup might not be enough."

I mixed everything together and put it in the microwave. "You could buy me an espresso." I beamed at her.

I was once again ignored. "We've got a job," she said.

"One of your special clients?" Which oftentimes meant illegal. "I thought you were taking December off before opening your new PI business."

The microwave dinged. Coffee in hand, I took a long drink before sliding onto a stool across from Fab.

"It's for Brick." She waved me off before I could yell, oh maybe, *Heck no.* "It's a car retrieval."

Brick Famosa was Fab's oldest and sleaziest client. He owned a high-end sports car dealership in South Miami, along with a handful of other cash businesses.

"Car retrieval" was fancy talk for repo job. It wouldn't be our first recovery, and not a one of them had gone off without incident. "Another cash car rental that didn't get returned?" He'd supposedly gotten out of that end of the business. "I thought you were on his do-not-call list." He hadn't called in a while, which pleased me. I'd almost managed to forget about him.

"A relative that didn't return a loaner."

"The last relative he sicced us on was a thief. I'm happy, for a number of reasons, that I'm not a member of that family. Which relative this time?"

"He hemmed and hawed." At my arched brow, she said, "I know — red flag. Finally told me it didn't matter."

"The punch line is — " I jumped up, " — ta da." And sat back down, laughing at her disgruntled look.

"The Ferrari is out in the Alley."

"A Ferrari to a relative? First red flag. Alley as in Alligator Alley? Clearly the punch line." Fab nodded. "Hell, no. Not going. Forget it," I said, ending in a near shout.

"Calm down. I don't want to go either."

"The reason he called you, in my humble estimation, is that he couldn't find anyone else to do the job and probably wouldn't put the life of that Amazon assistant of his in danger." I took a deep breath to calm down. The man had nerve. "How did you leave it?"

She hesitated so long, I ordered, "Pick up your phone now and tell him to stick the job."

"Triple pay."

As if those two words said it all. "You know that means bullets, and you can't spend the dough if you're dead."

"Your attitude isn't helpful. At least come up with a Plan B."

The cats awoke from one of their many naps and strolled single-file into the kitchen, Jazz leading the way, howling. Her usual ladylike self, Snow followed without a word. She knew Jazz could ramp up the drama all on his own and get them fed fast. The two chubby oldsters never missed a meal.

"My backup plan is the same as my original one—tell him no. I highly doubt this is one of his relatives."

Fab nodded, which amped up my radar. I

wondered what was going through that mind of hers.

"I'm leaving." I stood. "I've got to check on The Cottages since Mac hasn't found a replacement for her Mrs. Claus gig. And Doodad wants a meeting. He's never asked for one before. I told him I wanted assurances that he wasn't quitting or I wouldn't be in until January."

"I'm coming." She stood, grabbed the mugs, and crossed to the sink.

"Your job?"

"I told Brick I had to think about it and would call him later. Surprised me when he didn't end with a snide comment."

That right there was worrisome—the man always had a comeback.

Fab pulled into the driveway of The Cottages, parking in front of the office. Mac's truck was parked in front of Joseph's door, and he leaned against the back bumper in his elf suit, dragging on a cigarette, getting ready to light another off the end of the old one.

Mrs. Claus came around the corner from Crum's, alternately tugging on her apron and fiddling with a white-haired wig, a poofy elastic bonnet in her hand. She bent over to smooth out her tights; then, becoming aware of Fab and I heading her way, she waved.

"I don't like that outfit." Fab wrinkled her nose.

"My guess is that the kids don't care," I said. "Don't you remember sitting on Santa's lap? It's a fun memory to look back on. If you forget, you get a picture to remind you."

"Never did the Santa thing."

Hmm… My guess was her Christmases past were all grown-up affairs. I didn't want to ask because it gave me an idea for a surprise of my own.

"Where's Crum?" I asked.

Mac straightened up and jerked Joseph's cigarette out of his mouth, grinding it under her shoe. She'd accented her costume with colorful lights, which framed her pockets and wrapped around the straps of her black Mary Janes. She pointed to Crum's cottage. "Don't upset him. He's got five minutes; then we've got to leave for work."

"How are you doing?" I patted Joseph's shoulder.

"I'm having a good time." He hacked. "Would be better if there weren't any kids."

Mac clapped Joseph on the back hard enough that he dislodged something into the bushes.

I turned in time to see Crum's head disappear back inside the bathroom window, so I went over and knocked on his door.

"You're not in jail," I stated the obvious when

he opened the door in Santa pants, an undershirt, and suspenders, the most clothes I'd ever seen him in.

He motioned me inside, poking his head back out and looking both ways before closing the door. "If the cops come back, I'm going to need a lawyer. You got a referral? And not your lawyer, Cruz. His snotty secretary told me he didn't practice down here."

I sat down next to Harlot, asleep in her usual place on the couch, and scratched her neck, running my fingers through her fur. "The mention of your name probably brought up images of you doing the naked tango with his grandmother." I shook my head. "I'll text you the number of Ruthie Grace. She's local and not put off by folks operating on half-load."

Crum straightened to his full height of well over six feet. "I'll have you know—"

I cut him off before he could launch into a tirade about who had the higher IQ. We both knew it was him. "I know you're smarter than everyone in the Keys, but that doesn't mean you should be let out of the house by yourself."

"As much as fun as this has been—" He sniffed. "—I've got to get to work, reassure the kiddies I'll be at their house on Christmas Eve, and remind them not to forget the cookies. Mall management heard me tell one kid to lose the milk and ixnayed me saying that again. You'd have thought I asked for scotch."

"You need to stick to the script." With a last ear rub for the cat, I stood and headed for the door.

Crum grabbed a red jacket and black belt and followed me out.

Before walking out the door, I turned and asked, "Did Kevin say why you're a suspect?"

"I'm the only Santa in town."

"Until this person is caught—and they will be, sooner or later—make sure you can account for your time. Alibis are always good. It would help if your witnesses weren't known drunks."

He patted the top of my head. "Thanks for everything... stuff... whatever."

I debated either kicking him or laughing and did neither. "Stuff to you too. Have a good day." I motioned to Fab to get a move on. "You need anything, call," I said to Mac. I noticed the glare she sent at Fab. I'd find out what that was about when we got in the car.

Fab and I waited and watched as they all climbed in Mac's truck and she pulled out of the driveway.

"What did you do to Mac?" I asked as soon as Fab turned onto the main highway, headed to Jake's.

"Mac likes her job at the mall, but she's worried about the office and all the activity that goes on at the property. I thought she was asking me to take over, but after she had a good laugh, she said I didn't have the people skills. She wanted to know if I knew anyone that could sub in for a few days."

"Don't worry, I'll handle it. And I'll keep my fingers crossed that Mac finds a replacement Mrs. Claus quickly."

Fab flew into the parking lot of Jake's. Coming to a screeching halt, she flipped up the visor, looking out the windshield. "What have you done?"

"I did a little decorating, Ms. Grinch. If you give it a chance, it's going to look spectacular at night." The entire lot had been draped with colorful Christmas lights. Could it be overdone? Probably, but I liked it anyway.

"Even my lighthouse." She turned her head, scoping out the property.

In addition to the bar, the block also housed the lighthouse, now used as office space during the week and a tourist attraction on weekends. There was also a roach coach, Twinkie Princesses, which was never open. I'd left a phone message for them to get in the holiday spirit, and two nights later, the mobile kitchen had been draped in lights with a star on top. Junker's, a garden antiques dealer—some would say junk, but not in front of me—had been decorated since October.

Tired of Fab's slack-jawed expression, I got out

of the SUV and slammed the door, walking into the bar and down to the far end, where I slid onto a stool. "I'll have a Shirley Temple with plenty of cherries." At Doodad's amused look, I said, "Too early to get my drunk on."

"Where's your sidekick?"

"She's outside, overwhelmed by my ostentatious display of lights."

"Saw it lit up last night, and it looks good." He gave me a thumbs up. "I like them in here too; I think we should keep them up year round. It's not like this is a classy joint."

"Just take down the tree." I nodded to where it stood in the corner. "Since you're not quitting, what's up?"

"I'd like to do a theme night or two each week until New Year's. It's late for advertising, but I know a guy at the local throwaway, and we could get some free pimping. Maybe litter the town with flyers. Word of mouth and the locals will bring more locals, and hopefully some tourists."

"How much effort would I have to put in?"

"Put into what?" Fab asked, sliding onto a stool next to me. She picked up the glass Doodad had set in front of me and sniffed it.

"She can't have one; she's driving," I said.

Fab took a sip and spit it back in the glass. "That's terrible."

I glared at Doodad for laughing his silly head off. "You spit on my cherries. They're ruined."

"I'm sorry."

"No, you're not. I'm going to tell on you."

That made Doodad laugh harder. He whisked the glass away. "What are you drinking?" he asked Fab.

"Can you somehow make a soda and lime taste like a double martini?"

It took a minute before he set our drinks down in front of us. "I've got it all handled," he said to me.

"Just remember, keep the gunfire to a minimum and the cops here for pleasure rather than business."

"You might want to relax your rules a little. Sure, a bar fight clears out the place, especially when it comes with the sound of approaching sirens. But the next few nights, they're back, knee-deep, wanting to rehash events that they were never a part of. Which is good for your bottom line and my tip jar."

"Is someone going to tell me what's going on?" Fab demanded.

"Don't look at me," I said, pulling a cherry off one of the palm tree toothpicks we'd recently ordered.

After a glare-down between Fab and Doodad, he broke down and told her.

"Good idea," she said.

"Let me know the dates and themes. I want to be here for at least the first one," I said.

"This Saturday." Doodad pulled a flyer out

from behind the bar and handed it to me.

"Costume party—holiday beach attire," I read. "Prizes? What are they?"

"We've got three. First place: three free drinks. Second place: one drink. Third place: a token for the jukebox."

Fab turned up her nose. "Who thought those prizes up?"

"Where's your sense of fun?" I asked. "Our clientele won't care—they'll jump into the spirit of the festivities."

Doodad knuckle-bumped me.

Chapter Five

Fab rounded the corner to the house on one tire. Not really, but it felt like it. My cry of "slow down" went through her ears without a second's pause for recognition.

"It's Santa," I said, pointing. "Is that on my property?" The eight-foot inflatable Santa stood to one side of the driveway, one arm in a perpetual wave, ropes anchoring it to the palm tree. "Where did it come from?" I hopped out before Fab could cut the engine.

Tropical Santa had on a pair of bathing trunks, a Hawaiian shirt patterned with red and white hibiscuses, a red hat, white beard, and black flip-flops. Behind him, also secured to the tree, was a surfboard that matched his shirt.

I stood in awe, walking from side to side, gently touching him—he'd been filled with just the right amount of air. I eased off the envelope taped to his leg and opened it, withdrawing the card. "Ohhh…" I squealed, turning to find Fab, who'd stayed by the driver's door. I ran to her and threw my arms around her. "You're so amazing." I hugged her tight. "Love Santa. Love you."

"Get off me," she grumbled. "I can't breathe." She coughed, an exceptionally bad imitation. "You're so into Christmas; I wanted to do something you'd remember."

I grabbed her arm and dragged her back to the sidewalk. "And look—lights." I pointed to the strands running vertically behind Santa.

"You're giving me a headache."

"We need pictures," I said, full of excitement. "Lots and lots of pictures." I reached out to hug her again.

She held her hands out to ward me off. "Control yourself or I'll take it back."

"I can't wait to see it lit up at night."

"You want me to get you a beach chair so you can sit out here?"

"Get four. All of us can sit out here and wave to the neighbors."

She laughed, giving me a look that said it would never happen.

"Best present ever." I beamed at her and finally followed her into the house.

It wasn't until we were standing in the entry that I remembered seeing the guys' cars parked across the street. Didier was in the kitchen, head in the refrigerator, offering a nice view of his muscular backside.

I kicked off my shoes and turned into the kitchen. "Did you see Santa?"

"He's hard to miss." Didier chuckled. "Your light guy had a small air compressor in the back of his van, which meant we didn't have to unpack him at the gas station and then figure out how to get him back here." He winked at Fab, then dragged her to his side, planting a kiss on her head.

I grabbed a bottle of water from the refrigerator and held it out to Fab. She nodded, and I handed it off, grabbing another one. "Why are the French doors closed?" I peered into the living room. The cats were asleep on the daybed, instead of their favorite place just inside the doors to the patio.

"You are not to go out there," Didier ordered in a no-nonsense tone.

Fab stepped in front of me, blocking me from heading in that direction.

"Another surprise?" I flashed Fab a huge smile.

She shrugged. "Not in on this one. Neither Didier nor Creole would tell me what they're up too."

The patio door opened, and Creole poked his head inside. "What's taking so long?" He looked at me and Fab. "You two…" he said.

Creole and Didier exchanged a look.

I needed a class in guy code—they weren't as easy to read as Fab.

"I told them," Didier said.

Creole crossed the room and dropped a kiss on my lips. "You promise not to come out until we say?" I nodded. "You," he said to Fab. "Promise Didier."

I almost laughed at her look of frustration.

Creole motioned for Didier to join him. "Since you two are in the kitchen, why don't you rustle us up some dinner?" The guys laughed as they headed back to the patio.

The look Fab shot Creole should've at least singed his eyebrows.

I took up the challenge. "Dinner at six, and we're eating outside."

When the door closed, Fab asked, arms crossed, "Why did you offer to cook?"

"Who said the word cook?" I looked around. "Not me." I pulled my phone out of my pocket. "I'm ordering from Jake's and having it delivered. Cook's testing some new items I haven't had a chance to sample."

The guys came back in the house before the deadline.

"Ready for you," Didier announced.

Creole took a scarf from his back pocket and twirled it around before tying it around my eyes. "I've got you," he said, gripping my arm and leading me forward.

The first thing I heard after crossing the threshold was the sound of Christmas music coming through the speakers. We continued for several feet across the patio before coming to a halt.

"Surprise!" Fab yelled from behind me, which made me jump and then laugh.

Creole untied the scarf.

"So beautiful." I clapped my hands to my cheeks, staring up at the tallest Christmas tree I'd ever seen. "You grinches, it was all an act." I kissed Creole and whispered, "You wait until later." I ran over to Didier and hugged him and kissed his cheek.

"How tall is it?" Fab asked as she snapped pictures.

"Twelve feet," Creole told her. "With any luck, we can get it back in the box and use it next year."

"Looks real." I ran my hand over the branches. "Good choice. Just the right amount of lights. And decorations. You two were busy." I walked around the tree. "Great place to hide if we get an intruder."

Creole shook his head. "Let's hope that doesn't happen. No clue how many ornaments we'd need—came out on the short side."

"It's perfect," I said. "If we want more, we'll make it a tradition to add new ones every year."

"Doorbell?" Didier headed inside.

"It's the dinner I cooked," I said to his retreating back.

"Where do you want the food?" Creole asked.

"Bring it out here. Fab and I can set the table,

and we can enjoy the newest addition."

He nodded and followed Didier inside.

"They did a good job," Fab said.

"Yes, they did, and so did you." I hugged her again.

"Enough already. You need to set the table. I'll do my part and supervise."

I'd planted some little mini-poinsettias for centerpieces, and so far, they had remained in hearty shape. Opening a nearby cupboard, I pulled out some red dishes and silverware, hurriedly setting the table.

When dinner was over, I refilled the red enamelware bucket with ice and added more beers. I picked up the pitcher of what was left of my margaritas and set both the bucket and pitcher on the table just as Fab said something nice to Creole. That had my antenna on high alert, as he hadn't done anything specific and she typically didn't hand out compliments.

Sitting next to Creole, I finished off what was left of my drink. Creole reached for the pitcher and refilled my glass.

"You said if I ever needed backup for a job that you'd help out," Fab said to Creole.

"This is about Brick's job, isn't it?" I glared at her over the rim of my glass, then set it down, not quite a slam but close enough. "Forget it." I

48

pounded my fist on the table. "In case I'm not being clear—" I leaned in her direction. "—Creole's not going. And neither is Didier."

"They're grown men and can decide for themselves," Fab fumed.

"I'm well aware of what they are," I said. "Having learned a lot from their bossy ways, I'm ripping a page from their book. Not. Going. Don't think you're going to sneak one of them out behind my back either. That will force me to track you down and shoot *you* in the butt, and maybe nick them just because they didn't pay attention and decided to ignore me."

"When have I ever *nicked* you?" Creole asked in mock outrage, amusement lighting up his eyes.

"It's fortunate for our relationship that you haven't resorted to such tactics." I smiled sweetly.

Fab glared at Didier, who stared down at the label on his beer bottle, shoulders shaking.

"Calm down. I've got a Plan B," Fab said in exasperation.

Testing the waters? I bet Fab didn't think her biggest hurdle would be me.

"Why don't you run it by all of us?" I suggested sarcastically. "We'll take a group vote, and in the spirit of putting all the cards on the table, my vote counts double the guys'. Ready? This should be fun."

If looks could kill, I'd have been toes up.

Didier raised his hand. "Sounds good to me."

Creole nodded. "Whatever the boss says."

"I'm sure the guys are wondering what the heck you're talking about," I said to Fab. "So I'll start with the short version, and you fill in the details. This is that Brick case — sports car that didn't get returned — and let's not forget the phony relative story," I added in disgust.

Fab relayed the particulars, barely adding to what I'd already said. "Plan B — and since contracting out my jobs was your idea, I'm sure you'll approve — " The smile she gave me lacked sincerity. " — I thought this would be a good job to hand off to one of my associates and see how it goes."

"That should've been Plan A." I finished off the rest of my second, or maybe third, margarita, half-stood, and glared down at her. "You're lucky I don't pull your hair out."

Fab downed the last of her martini and put her dukes in the air.

Creole grabbed the back of my skirt, pulling me back into my chair.

"*Ladies,* as much fun as… well, never mind." Didier laughed. "This isn't WWF fight night."

Palms on the table, I said, "You better point out *all* of the pitfalls to the unsuspecting schlub."

"Got it." Fab saluted.

"Another drink, anyone?" I asked, sticking my glass in the air.

Fab raised her martini glass, hanging it upside down.

Creole pushed my hand down.

"You two have been cut off." Didier laughed.

Chapter Six

Fab rocketed into the parking lot of the Tropical Slumber Funeral Home. The lot was empty — even the hearse had been put away. She parked practically on the lawn. "Why are we the only ones here?" she asked.

The decorations had been found. Well, sort of. The husband-and-wife thieves had been caught in the act of stealing from another neighbor. Their excuse was they needed the items to decorate their own yard. Several of the inflatables matched the pictures that Dickie and Raul had taken, but another couple was also making a claim, which would make it impossible for the police to determine the rightful owner.

When Raul had called yesterday with the news that they wouldn't be decorating this year, his disappointment rang through the phone. He'd tried to hire a service, because he and Raul couldn't do it by themselves, but they were all booked.

I'd thrown out the idea of getting as many people as we could to bring one decoration apiece and stay to help get the front lawn back into shape. My thought was, with enough people, it could be done in a few hours. Today had turned out to be the best choice since no funerals were scheduled. It was Dickie's idea to offer food and drinks.

"I called everyone I know, laid on the guilt and arm-twisted to get people here to help the guys out. I was annoyed with the lackluster response I got. And you?" I asked.

Fab and I had just come from Junker's, and the back of the SUV was loaded with a hodge-podge of outside decorations.

"I told Didier, and he laughed at me. I'm not sure he believed me."

"The guys snuck off this morning, like we wouldn't notice. If that was their way of saying they don't want to help, I'll have plenty to say about that later. It's hard to believe that they'd be a no-show. Even though they both commented that this place creeps them out." I went around and opened the back door, dragging out a cardboard box of reindeer inflatables and a sleigh that Junker had hidden in the corner and nearly forgotten about. He'd been about to jack up the price in his typical style, but his seldom-seen wife insisted we just take them, since they couldn't guarantee the condition.

Originally, Fab and I had decided to purchase a snowman family as our contribution, but when we went to pick it up, Fab had added Santa on a motorcycle and I'd tossed in Mickey and Minnie Mouse.

A sheriff's car pulled in and parked next to the SUV. Kevin got out. "Who died?"

"You're not funny," I said. He flashed a pouty face. "We could use some help carrying this stuff."

"You should've driven up on the lawn." Kevin looked over his shoulder. "Besides, I'm here on official business."

"Dead body in the trunk?" Fab asked, enjoying his look of annoyance.

"I'm coming," Dickie yelled from the garage area. He started running, pushing an out-of-control hand truck.

"He's going to fall down." I shuddered and held my breath until he skidded to a stop in front of us.

"Officer," Dickie said, out of breath.

"I've got an update on your theft case," Kevin said.

"Let me go get Raul." Dickie raced off.

"Energetic fellow."

"Since when does law enforcement make house calls of this type?" I asked.

"Apparently, there *is* something that you're the last to know. Those two—" He nodded at the two men crossing the parking lot. "—are good friends with the sheriff. Like this." He crossed his fingers. "I was curious what they had in common but figured there was no good way to ask without coming off as a dick."

Before the two men rejoined us, Fab and I had

moved all the boxes out of the back of the SUV and onto middle of the lawn with Kevin's help.

"You don't look very happy—more bad news?" Raul asked.

"Kevin's always a grouch," Fab mumbled, but we all heard.

"You want to take this inside?" Kevin asked.

"We have nothing to hide from Fab and Madison." Raul smiled at Fab.

"The Mathis couple did steal your inflatables. I found your markings on the bottoms, just where you said they'd be. That gives us a good case against them. According to the wife, her husband went on a drunken tear and… well… he vandalized a few of them beyond repair." Kevin shifted uncomfortably.

"Mathis?" I asked, trying to recall where I'd heard the name. After a moment, I remembered. "Isn't that the seventeen-year-old who married the forty-year-old woman?"

"That's them." Kevin grimaced. "I checked it out, and turns out, he got a note from his mom, so it was legal. I'm certain it was true love. When I showed up the second time, the wife threw her husband under the bus with lightning speed, claiming he was the brains of the operation."

"She skated?" I asked.

"Oh no, she got hauled in and released on bail. Lover boy tried to escape custody by running, hands cuffed behind his back. I waited for him to fall, which he did after a couple of steps, and then hauled him in for booking. He also got bail, but apparently they only had enough assets for one of them to be released."

"Why don't you stick around and help with the redecoration?" Fab asked in a challenging tone.

"The goal is to have it decorated by the end of the day," I said.

"The four of you?" Kevin asked. "As you can see, I'm on duty."

I shot him a dirty look.

"Thanks to these two—" Raul smiled at Fab and me. "—several boxes of decorations arrived this morning, and we got them laid out." He pointed to the lawn. "The display will be a little smaller, but since we have a ton of lights, that will fill in any holes."

Three pickup trucks rolled into the parking lot, the first two with men in the back, some of them familiar faces from Jake's. The last one had me smiling—Creole and Didier had shown up, and Liam jumped out of the back, along with a... dog? A German Shepherd, in fact.

The family had adopted Liam when his mother dated my brother. Even though that relationship had ended, we still considered him an official member of the family.

"What is that? Besides the obvious," I asked, pulling Liam into a hug. "Can you have animals at school?"

"Left school this morning and hit the gas

station. While I was there, a car pulled to the side of the road, dog hopped out to do his business, and the car took off. I got the license number, but I don't want them getting the dog back. I'll find it a home while I'm here on winter break." Liam was spending part of his break from the University of Miami in the Cove before jetting off to be with his mom in California for the holidays.

I turned in time to see Creole and Didier smirking at me. I could read their minds—no dogs. "We'll find him a good home." I smiled at Liam, then down at the dog, who sat patiently between us. "You think he's hungry?"

"I stopped and got him two double burgers and a couple of large waters."

"Did you actually manage to sneak a big dog into Mother's condo?"

"She was cool about it once I assured her I'd be finding him a home."

"Does she know that you and the dog are out gallivanting around?" He lived at Mother's when not away at school, and she watched him like a hawk and rarely let him out of her sight.

"Grandmother went to do errands before I got the call to contribute my brawn." Liam flexed his muscles. "I left a note."

Astro and Necco came around the back of the main building. They spotted "Dog" at the same time he spotted them, did a double take, and the three raced towards each other.

"Go be a dog wrangler and make sure nothing

bad happens," I said to Liam, who started off after them.

After a thorough sniff, a chase ensued, including barking and jumping. One of the Dobermans raced off and came back with a Frisbee that he dropped at Liam's feet. Liam started throwing it and soon had them running in circles.

I overheard Dickie offer Kevin food, telling him he'd set up a buffet in the main room, where all the services took place. Kevin shook his head. I was certain it was because he didn't want to go inside if he didn't have to.

"I have to get back to work," he said.

"I can prepare a plate, and you can take it with you," Dickie offered.

Kevin readily agreed.

Dickie turned to go. "Kevin likes Coke," I called. He nodded.

Kevin turned on me, I figured to complain about my sticking my nose in his business, and I scooted around him and headed straight to Creole, who was already organizing the men piling out of the trucks, one driven by Mac and the other by Doodad. Didier scooped Fab off her feet, twirling her around.

Dickie had set up a wide variety of cold sodas and bottled waters in bins filled with ice under a large tiki umbrella in the middle of the patio. Raul shepherded everyone over, and they helped themselves before going to work. Two air compressors and a generator had been unloaded off one of the trucks and were now being used to blow up the various pieces. A small assembly line formed, tying string and pounding in stakes.

After checking the design drawing Raul had taped to the table, I picked up a handful of candy canes, took them to the taped-off area, and poked them into the ground.

"I don't know what you promised your guys to get them to show up," Fab told Mac, "but I'll cover the tab. You can always be counted on."

From the look on Mac's face, I knew the compliment meant everything to her. She had a never-ending girl crush.

With fifteen men showing up, a third of them natural leaders, the lawn went together in record time. It wasn't ostentatious like the first display, but it looked darn good, and when the lights were turned on, everyone clapped.

Chapter Seven

"Party time!"

Creole lifted and whirled me around in the doorway of Jake's. I had on a red tankini bathing suit, a red-dyed grass skirt that had faded in spots, and red-and-white leis around my neck. After some grumbling, Creole had agreed to wear the Santa-face bathing trunks I'd purchased. He'd also chosen a black tropical shirt, which he left unbuttoned, and I'd added matching leis around his neck.

Fab rocked the hula-girl look—green grass skirt with colorful fabric hibiscus flowers fastened around her waist. Her bra top was made from coconut shells adorned with the same flower, and she'd finished off her outfit with flowery wristbands. Didier sported a pair of red board shorts and a white dress shirt.

Being the owner of a dive bar had perks, and I'd reserved the outside deck for friends, and possibly a family member or two, if they were brave enough to show up. Since my mother got married, her interest in coming to Jake's had waned. My brother had sniffed that Jake's didn't have the proper ambience for a cigar and scotch.

Then he'd winked at me. But I refused to miss Jake's first costume bash.

Unlocking the doors to the deck, I flipped on the ceiling fans and the lights that ran along the deck railing and the edge of the roof. The usual white ones had been replaced with multi-colored ones, the space reconfigured into one long table. Most of the seats offered a good vantage point for watching the comings and goings inside the bar.

Mac blew through the door, bending down to whisper, "Crum got arrested." It came out as more of a shout. Conversation came to a halt.

Eye-level with her chest, which was coming dangerously close to spilling out of her bathing suit top, I leaned back before asking, "What happened?" I glanced down at her tree skirt, made out of felt with large round circles that I assumed were ornaments glued on. Strings of lights around her neck and elf shoes with bells on the toes put the finishing touch on her outfit.

"Bank robbery." She made a second attempt at a whisper and failed. "Big-time felony. Though he swears he didn't do it. I believe him, but the cops didn't ask my opinion."

I don't know why she wouldn't speak in her normal voice, using her chain-smoker voice instead. And she didn't even smoke. Besides, she had everyone's rapt attention.

"Is he going to get bail?" I asked Mac, at the same time shrugging at Fab, silently asking, *Do we have a bondsman?*

Mac answered my unspoken question. "Counselor Grace is on it. Didn't complain one bit when I called after hours, and she assured me she'd be heading to the police station immediately. Then referred me to some guy I swear she called 'Barndoor.' Turns out its Bar*nard*, and he's got zero sense of humor."

Both Creole and Didier laughed.

"Why are you calling her 'counselor'?" Fab asked.

"She says it sounds chic. Besides, 'Ruthie' is a little forward. I'd like to offer her a free meal — I think she's a Jake's kind of gal."

I wasn't sure that was a compliment but nodded. If I hadn't already had Ruthie Grace checked out, I would do it now. The report had come back showing a stellar reputation and impressive win record. That made up for a little eccentricity.

"Here's another title for your resume," I said to Mac. "Bail arranger."

She grinned at that idea. Doodad set a bottle of beer in front of her and delivered the rest of the drinks I'd pre-ordered.

"Can't party until the fun arrives," Liam said from the doorway. "Here I am." He'd joined in the spirit, showing up in green bathing trunks, a U-logo t-shirt from school, and an elf hat with ears, a large jingle bell on the tip.

"You sneak out again?" Didier asked Liam,

giving him a thumbs up on the outfit.

Liam made a face. "Not exactly. The Spoons went out for dinner, and I left another note and caught a cab over here. The note thing works good for me. No longwinded explanations necessary."

"Mother must've done something if you're calling her Mrs. Spoon," I said.

"We had a 'discussion' about how she packed my calendar full of activities until I leave to go visit Mom in California. I went through and crossed most of it out, telling her I needed time to do nothing and had a few invitations of my own. This being one of them." Liam claimed the chair that Creole pointed him to.

"Find a home for the dog yet?" Didier asked.

"Yep," Liam said smugly. "Good one too."

"You going to tell us?" Fab asked.

"Nope." He shook his head. "He had a temporary home for a couple of days and then got his forever home. I'll let those responsible tell you."

Someone we know? That made me mildly nervous, but I knew Liam would make sure the dog had a good home and would never be left on the side of the road again.

Doodad came back, large platter in hand, followed by Dickie and Raul. Fab hopped up and greeted them. It surprised me that they'd come, as I didn't often see the two outside the funeral home.

"The bar's filling up. Your idea was a good one," I said to Doodad as he set the array of appetizers down. Another special order I'd arranged.

"Just fired the new guy. Smoking a bowl in the middle of the kitchen isn't cool. He shouldn't be doing it at work... or should at least wait for his break and go out to his car. We need to write that we drug test on the bottom of the application—that will scare some of them off."

"I'm the last to know we even *have* an application." I tried not to laugh.

"I meant it in the cosmic sense of... I'm just full of it." He walked off.

Mac pushed her chair back and chased after Doodad, grabbing his arm.

A loud crash, followed by a second, softer one, brought all conversation, inside and out, to a halt. Creole flew out of his seat, Didier behind him, and they ran into the bar. Doodad and Liam followed.

The patrons' eyes were fixed on the front door. I stood on a chair to improve my view. From what I could see, it looked like the front end of a golf cart had gotten wedged in the doorframe. The reindeer tied to the top hung lopsided. There'd been a local parade earlier—decorate your cart in the spirit of the season, anyone could enter. But that didn't answer the question of how it got here, now probably totaled.

Creole came back in via the rear entrance and

waved me over. I was surprised Fab hadn't followed the guys to check out the scene, instead staying behind to talk to Raul and Dickie.

"Two drunk men in golf carts came up with the bright idea of drag racing. Eyewitnesses said they were driving around in circles in the parking lot when one guy's engine died. The other guy, either on purpose or because he wasn't paying attention, rear-ended him, propelling him through the doorway... partially, anyway." Creole shook his head in disbelief.

"Anyone hurt?" I asked.

"No, and thank goodness they didn't take out any bystanders. There are a few of them out there, snapping pics, taking video, or both."

"What can I do?"

"Stay in here and have fun. I got some men together to pull the cart out of the doorway. Didier says he can send a carpenter over tomorrow to fix the damage. Doesn't think it's as bad as it looks."

Someone inside had chosen "Ho, Ho, Ho and a Bottle of Rum" on the jukebox and started singing along to the Jimmy Buffet tune. That was the signal that the drama was no longer interesting.

"You pressing charges?" Creole asked.

"I probably shouldn't admit this, but I never do. And yet the cops manage to show up anyway."

"I'll take care of it." He flexed his muscles. "I

know a couple of local cops. Hopefully one of them is working and we can get this cleaned up quickly."

"You were a good catch." I stood on tiptoes and kissed him.

"Except I was the one to bait the hook and reel you in." He cast a line with his invisible fishing rod.

Remembering that Doodad was outside, I veered toward the bar, not believing he'd leave it unattended but needing to check it out. *So that's where Mac disappeared to.*

"Need help?" I called to her.

She waved me away, sliding two beers down the bar.

It didn't take long before the guys had extracted the cart from the opening and pushed it into a parking space. One of the drivers called a cab, and they both hopped in and left before the cops arrived. That wouldn't keep them out of trouble, as Creole had gotten their information, letting them know they'd be paying the repair bill.

Creole, Didier, and Liam returned to the table. Didier suggested a toast but got interrupted by loud voices as the sounds of an argument drifted out the door.

What now?

Just inside the double doors, two women were wrestling in a circle of onlookers, pulling each other's hair, slapping the air, and shrieking.

I wagered, "A dollar says they're both sleeping with the same guy and they just found out."

"I'll take that bet," Liam said. "How are you going to find out?"

"We'll send Fab—she's the PI." I laughed at the glare she sent me.

Doodad came out from behind the bar and bravely stepped between the two women, yelling, "Shut it!" He gripped an arm in each hand and led them towards the back exit.

"What was the fight about?" Liam asked eagerly when he came back.

"Trash talking," Doodad said, like he couldn't believe it. "Who's better looking, who's got the bigger boobs... They're regulars and always starting stuff."

"You owe me a dollar," Liam told me.

I nudged Creole. "Can you front me the money?"

"Just so you know, I charge interest, and no complaining when it's time to pay up."

I leaned over and kissed his cheek. "Deal."

"I'm getting ready to award prizes. You want to be the one to present them?" Doodad asked me.

I shook my head. "How about Fab? She's the outgoing one."

"I'll do it," Liam volunteered. "It's going to be easy since over half didn't come in a costume. Bathing suit trunks don't count." He stared at

Creole and Didier, letting them know they didn't make the cut. "Only the women made much of an effort." He stood and followed Doodad into the bar. Circling the room several times before claiming the microphone, he made a showy spectacle of approaching each winner and awarding their prize. When Liam finished, all of us on the deck clapped, to which he responded with a bow.

The rest of the evening went off without a glitch. We ate and drank until everyone at the table was stuffed. The mountain of food that had been delivered was devoured.

Raul announced that they had found a home for Polar, the rescued dog's new name. Polar resembled a dog they'd buried in their pet cemetery, whose owner had taken his companion's death hard. The older man had resisted adopting another dog, but when presented with the homeless animal, he'd jumped at adopting the German Shepherd. The guys had helped him research holiday-themed animal names, and he liked that one best. Since the three dogs got along so well, it was decided that Polar would be back for play dates.

"The dogs can jump around in the mud again," Raul said sardonically.

At the opposite end of the table, Dickie stood up, placing a shopping bag on the table. "Raul and I want to thank you for your help in the decoration fiasco. To make sure it doesn't happen again, we got advice on how to secure everything. So, a small gift from us to you." He reached into the bag, withdrawing some small red boxes that Raul distributed to the women. Next came green boxes, and they went to the men. "A useful reminder of your Tropical Slumber experience."

The red brocade pattern on the box reminded me of the furniture in the funeral home, and I was loath to touch it. I leaned my head against Creole's shoulder. "You first."

"I don't want to."

"Me neither."

"Since we don't want to hurt their feelings, on the count of three, we open at the same time."

I nodded. Fab caught our attention by opening hers and Didier's, seemingly at once. From the red box, she pulled out a silver pendant necklace in the shape of an old-fashioned bottle, and from the green one, blown-glass cuff links.

Mac, who'd returned to the table some time ago, had already opened her box. "That's right pretty," she cooed, pulling out an exact duplicate of Fab's necklace. "Now that's special." She dangled the necklace in front of her face.

"Thank you," I murmured, slipping the box, unopened, into my pocket.

Didier jerked his arm away when Fab tried to put one of the cufflinks on him, eyeing them suspiciously.

"This is very pretty. Thank you, Raul and

Dickie." Fab held up the necklace. "What's this?" She tapped the back side.

Raul stood, necklace in hand. "When a loved one dies and is cremated, remove the top—that's the opening." He demonstrated. "And fill with ashes. Same with the cufflinks. Make sure you get the closures secured. You will always have your loved one near."

An awkward hush fell over the table.

"You're a clever one," Didier said. He must have realized it didn't sound like a compliment and added, "Darn good idea."

"Well, I'll be." Mac bobbed her head. "I've got a couple of friends that are gift shop managers. I can show this to them—maybe they'll order some for their stores."

"That's sweet of you, but they're reserved for our clients," Dickie said.

I elbowed Creole gently in the side.

"Yeah, great idea," he said.

Liam leaned over and whispered, "I'm going to fill mine with dirt and tell the kids at school it's my Uncle Harry." At my incredulous look, he added, "Harry's made up, so no harm there."

Overhearing, Creole snorted.

I wasn't sure how it happened, but the rest of the night was uneventful.

Chapter Eight

"Crum's not in jail." I banged my phone on the counter. When I called the jail, they'd informed me he wasn't on their guest list. "He's also not answering his phone."

"He's a grown man and can take of his own legal problems." Fab scooped up my mug and hers, putting them in the dishwasher. "I know that's not going to stop you from getting involved." She took hold of my hand and ushered me into the entry, hooking my purse over my shoulder.

"Where are we going?" I asked as she shoved me out the door.

"The mall. Crum probably went to work. The older ladies with bad boy fantasies will be lining up."

Eww. "According to Mac, he dialed back his friendly attitude after mall management issued what they said was a final warning after a couple of women got in a shoving match. They said if any damage occurred during a fight over him, they'd hold him financially responsible."

"Did you know he's sending the lucky women home with his Santa business card?"

"I don't believe you." I turned and smirked out the window, wondering how long she'd held onto that tidbit, also knowing that the woman didn't make statements she couldn't back up.

"Check the side pocket of my purse." She pointed behind her as though I didn't know where she kept her purse.

"You better have gotten me one."

"There's a few in there, and no, I'm not passing them out. I figure when he runs out, I'll sell them to the ladies that didn't get one—at a premium price."

I laughed. "Please let me be there when Didier finds out about your latest entrepreneurial adventure."

"Being a naughty girl has its perks." She flashed a dreamy, self-satisfied smile.

"Stop." I crossed my fingers in front of me.

My phone rang. I retrieved it from the cup holder and answered, hitting the speaker button. "It's Mac."

"Heads up: Crum didn't come to work today. He got fired when management found out about his arrest. One of the maintenance men is filling in."

"You talk to him?"

"He didn't come back to The Cottages when he got released. Called me with an update this morning. Refused to say where he was staying. I asked him if he was on the run, and he sounded insulted while spitting out a denial."

"Anything else I should know about?"

"I found a replacement for my Mrs. Claus gig, and she starts tomorrow, so after that, you can find me in the office, the pool, or somewhere around."

"Just keep your phone turned on," Fab yelled.

Someone called Mac's name in the background. "Talk to you later," I said hurriedly before hanging up. "Let's go pay a visit to Crum's lawyer, Ms. Grace." I scrolled through the phone, getting the address. "It's not far from the funeral home."

"You're not wearing your necklace." Fab gave me a one-eyed once-over.

"Didn't go with my outfit." I shuddered at the thought of ever wearing it. "I'll point out the obvious—you're not wearing yours either."

Fab was quick, but not quick enough. I saw the edges of her mouth turn up before she changed the subject. "Do we have the nerve to show up at a law office without an appointment?"

I stared at her.

"What? It was an easy question."

"You must need a reminder. We have the nerve to do a lot of things."

Fab pulled up in front of six storefronts linked together, a door in the middle advertising office space upstairs. It was unclear if it was one of those rent-by-the-hour places one of Fab's associates had told me about once.

Ms. Grace had a unit with a private entrance at the end of the sidewalk. The picture window and door were shuttered, giving no indication whether she was open for business or not. I tried the door handle and found it locked.

"I can pick it," Fab offered.

"Probably not a good idea." I knocked politely.

"I was about to point out that if she wasn't opening the door, she wasn't here and say let's get out of here, but one of the shutters just moved. Most people probably wouldn't have noticed, but then, they're not me."

I looked down at my sandal-clad feet. "I don't have the right shoes on for this." Instead of kicking the bottom of the door, I banged on the door with my best cop knock. It sounded rusty to me but not enough to be noticeable. To drive home the message that we weren't going anywhere until she opened the door, I did it again.

The shutters flipped open. "What do you want?" the middle-aged, curly-haired redhead bellowed.

"Madison Westin." I pasted a smile on my face and waved. "If I need a recommendation, I'm Mac Lane's boss. Here about my tenant, Professor Crum."

"And her?" She indicated Fab.

"You could open the door, so we could stop yelling and use our quiet voices," I suggested, saying the latter in Mother's lecturing tone.

The side of her mouth curled up as she unlocked the door. "Five minutes, and then I start charging."

"Good luck collecting."

"I've got people."

"So do I."

Fab interrupted with a hand wave and a glare. "If you two are done with 'who's got the meaner, tougher group of hoodlums on call,' I'd like to sit. Counselor Grace, I assume? If not, you're wasting our time."

I almost laughed about Fab remembering the woman's preference for being called "counselor" since she professed not to remember name one.

Ms. Grace nodded. "You are?"

"Fabiana Merceau, the best PI in the Cove. Legal jobs only, grey areas can be negotiated."

"Never heard of you," Ms. Grace sniffed.

"You will when the billboard goes up."

I lowered my head, chest shaking, knowing that was an outrageous lie but liking the idea.

Ms. Grace waved us inside, and Fab closed the door. After pointing us to the chairs in front of her desk, the lawyer adjusted her short-sleeved tropical caftan before settling behind her desk.

Cute office, although white overload. The wainscoting got my approval, decorated in a beach theme. My shell collection was far more impressive than hers.

"Regarding the professor, he's a client and has

a right to confidentiality. Anything else?" Ms. Grace tapped her watch.

"I wanted to thank you for referring him to Mr. Barnard. I called the jail this morning and found out he'd been released."

She humphed with a slight smile. "He planned to post his own bail, since he had the wherewithal if necessary. Thankfully, it wasn't. Not sure any bondsman would write him a bond with his surly attitude. After a short conversation with my guy, during which Crum called him a 'nitwit' and excoriated him for his interest rates, not sure who hung up on the other first. But all's well, etc. Crum ended up getting released without charges, just an admonition not to leave town."

"We're here to offer our services. I've known Crum for a while, and I'm positive he's not out robbing banks." The only thing I knew he helped himself to that belonged to other people was their trash. The city hadn't made that a crime yet.

"Both of you are licensed?" Ms. Grace checked us out more carefully.

Fab raised her hand. "I'm licensed. This is my backup."

"The robber wore a pair of red bathing trunks, and an identical pair were found in Crum's locker at the mall. Any idea how they got there?" Ms. Grace asked with a flinty stare.

"If you had been at the costume party at Jake's, you'd have seen a dozen pairs of red bathing trunks. I take it they don't have anything like a fingerprint, eyewitness ID, or something more substantial?" I asked.

"The cops got a description from one of the bank customers, but it was generic enough to fit most men."

"The few times I've seen Crum leaving for work, he's half-dressed in his Santa pants and undershirt. You can verify with Mac since she's the designated driver. In his off hours, he finds clothes restricting." I ignored Fab's snort. "He favors tighty-whities. Due to a dress code that got imposed after he moved in, if he ventures outside, he must cover up, and he generally dons a bath towel that he rigged into a skirt and sometimes a shirt."

Ms. Grace picked up her soda and took a long swig, studying me over the top of the can. "Why would you rent to him?"

"I didn't. He was snuck in by my brother, but that's a story for another time."

"You two want to be useful, go down to that mall, get in the dressing room, and take pictures. My request for a tour was turned down this morning."

"Pictures are Fab's specialty, and just so you know, she's not squeamish about dead people." I glanced over at her and saw she'd leaned back in her chair, eyes closed. She was damn lucky she wasn't close enough for me to kick.

"So far, no one's been murdered. Like to keep

it that way," Ms. Grace said. "Generally, bail gets denied in homicide cases."

"Anything Crum needs, give me a call." I reached in my pocket, handing her one of Fab's business cards. Finally, one of us had gotten a professional-looking card.

Ms. Grace eyed the card before dropping it on her desk. "How does this partnership of yours work? You do all the talking while she sleeps."

"Trust me, she heard every word. Feel free to throw something at her; she'll catch it." I reached over and jerked the arm of Fab's chair. Her eyes popped open, patented smirk firmly in place. "Trust me, she's good when she's not doing her best to be annoying. As for me—I'm at her beck and call unless Beck is an ex-felon whose current partner has turned up dead. Besides, I've got interests of my own."

"This has been nice. Get me what I want, and we'll talk again." Left unsaid was *then this won't have been a complete waste of my time.* "I've got a brief to write." She flicked her finger through a pile of papers, a three-foot-thick book open off to one side.

"There is one more thing," I said, standing.

"Yes." It sounded more like "hurry up and get to the point."

"If we were in need of your services, would you take the call?" I asked.

That surprised her. "You don't already have a lawyer?"

"He doesn't like to come down to the Cove."

"I don't do freebies. Pro bono work on occasion, but only for a defendant in need." Giving it some thought, she added, "Call anytime."

"Could you be more annoying?" I hissed at Fab as the door closed behind us.

"You know the answer is yes." Fab slid behind the wheel of the SUV. "We'll go get the pictures and impress the heck out of her. That makes it easier to propose a trade for services."

"Now?" At Fab's nod, I suggested, "While I'm guarding the dressing room door, you sneak in. You'll know what she needs in the way of pictures."

"Good plan. I've got a hunch the bathing trunks in his locker will turn out to be a weird fluke, probably something Crum retrieved from the trash. If that's true, maybe he'll remember what bin he got them out of and his lawyer can get a statement."

"I'm hoping Mr. Bank Robber gets nabbed at his next stick-up."

Chapter Nine

As soon as I opened the front door, Fab scooted around me and went up the stairs. "I hope it tastes as good as it smells." I kicked off my shoes and crossed the living room and out the doors to the patio, putting my arms around Creole. "Shirtless and cooking, just the way I like you." I kissed his chest.

"I got the table set," Didier boasted from where he stood, finishing with the last of the silverware. "Where's Fab?" He walked over and poked his head through the patio doors.

"I'm right here," Fab called from the top of the stairs.

"Fabiana," Didier scolded, a note of laughter in his voice.

My guess was she'd slid down the bannister.

Fab came into view, laptop in hand, and paused before stepping outside. "I need to send some pictures." She headed for the table and set down her computer.

We took our assigned seats at the table. I found it amusing that we never changed it up. Didier poured Fab and me wine; he and Creole were drinking beer.

"How much trouble did you get into?" Creole asked, sitting next to me.

"We didn't get caught, so that doesn't count, does it?" I asked, feigning innocence.

Fab groaned and lifted the cover on her laptop, hiding her face behind the screen.

"Does that mean the cops will be here soon, warrant in hand?" Creole asked. I shook my head. "That's good."

"Another plus: no bullets or anyone chasing after us." I smiled.

"Stick to the facts," Fab grouched.

I updated them on Crum's case and detailed the conversation with his lawyer, including the information she wanted and said she couldn't get on her own. "I texted Mac ahead of time on how to gain access to the dressing room in case it was locked this time—the door has a combination lock. Didn't matter, though, as the door stood wide open. Crum's locker didn't have a padlock, and the big find there was a dirty towel."

Fab peered at us over her the top of her laptop. "I took pictures while Madison guarded the door. After that, I shot a couple of videos. Ms. Grace will soon have footage of every square inch."

"Bored with guard duty, and after checking to make sure the door was locked, I went around the small room and opened every door that didn't have a lock," I said. "Found nothing exciting. Candy wrappers, a few dead bugs."

"In and out, five minutes." Fab flexed her biceps.

Didier leaned down and kissed her arm.

"Getting out was just as easy as getting in," I said. "I poked my head out the door. The hallway was empty and stayed that way until we got to the end and made another turn, at which point, we mingled with people using the restrooms. No one paid us any particular attention. We exited through the food court and headed straight for the SUV."

Fab turned her laptop around, the screen filled with the pictures she'd taken. "You're the cop, what am I missing?" she asked Creole.

"I'd have been surprised if you'd found anything that would prove Crum's guilt or innocence. If it comes to mounting a defense, the lawyer can use these videos to show how readily accessible the area was, but I'm not sure how any of this relates to the bank robberies. The District Attorney can't make a case on Crum owning the same color trunks." Creole shook his head. "If that was all the evidence I had in a case, I'd be laughed out of the office."

"Didn't think about this before," I said, "but maybe Ms. Grace was testing your PI skills… or just wanted to get us out of her office."

"Crum needs to a keep a low profile," Didier suggested.

"My advice would be for him to stay away from banks, while in costume anyway," Creole half-laughed. "Now that he's been sacked, he needs to log where he's spending his time. That way, he'll know what his alibi is when the next robbery goes down."

"The Cottages is a good place to hang out," I said. "At least a half-dozen people are peering out their windows at any given time."

"I just sent everything to Ms. Grace," Fab said.

"Good. That means we can eat," I said.

Dinner over, the dishes cleared, we stayed around the table. The ringing of Fab's phone interrupted the conversation. She glanced briefly at the screen and hit the reject button. After a brief pause, it rang again.

"Whoever you're trying to avoid is persistent." I tried to get a look at the screen, but she flipped the phone over.

Creole nudged me in the side. Not even him actually saying "it's none of your business" would detour me.

"It's Brick," Fab said, exasperated. "He's not in a good mood right now."

"When is he ever?" I narrowed my gaze on her and knew instinctively that something was up. I also knew that if Brick was calling her repeatedly, it wouldn't be good news.

Knowing it would ring again, since the man never gave up, I was ready when it did and slid the phone to my side of the table. It surprised me that Fab only made a half-hearted attempt to stop me.

"Yeah," I said, doing my best to sound annoyed, which wasn't hard.

After a long pause, Brick barked, "Put Fab on."

"I'm sorry," I said in a sugary-sweet tone. "She ate something at lunch that didn't agree with her, and she's in the bathroom barfing. Would you care to hang on? It could be a while."

The guys never interfered in our dramas and weren't about to start now. They'd been watching with rapt interest, and both now had their heads down, shoulders twitching. If you could get them to cop to it, they enjoyed the little dramatic sideshows, but should it come to a smackdown, they'd be out of their chairs in a hot second. It wouldn't have surprised me if Brick could hear Fab's hiss from across the table.

After another few seconds, it sounded like he hung up. I double-checked the screen to make sure, though I wasn't surprised—he made a habit of disconnecting without a goodbye. I considered myself lucky he couldn't slam the thing down and blow out my eardrum.

"Brick won't be calling back tonight." I turned the phone off before setting it back on the table. "But don't think you'll get rid of him that easily. All this does is buy us time to come up with a plausible excuse for whatever you've done this time."

"For once, I didn't do a darn thing," she snapped. "And it's your job to handle customer complaints."

"Since you haven't officially offered me employment with your new company and there's no signed contract, that isn't actually my job. But I could handle it, just this one time." It was a good thing we were friends or she'd probably have shot me about then. "As we both know, I'm the one with the people skills. But despite that, you might still lose a few clients. That's why I want it stated in that contract that such incidents will be forgiven."

Creole and Didier threw their heads back and laughed.

"Drama Queen."

"If I were standing, I would curtsy. Next time I'm in the mood for that, I'll give you two." I flashed my crazy smile.

"This has been a great dinner." Fab smiled at Didier. "We can finish discussing this another time. How about a swim?"

I clapped. "Nice subject change. But it's not going to work. Now's the perfect time." Fab was mistaken if she thought a brush-off would deter me from learning whatever it was that had made Brick angry. "You might as well tell us all together. That way, none of the flavor of the story is lost in the retelling. Don't tell me you wouldn't want to know and now."

"It's about the Ferrari. It's been recovered," Fab said, clearly disgruntled at what should be good news.

"I'm sure the guys will be ecstatic, after whatever you're about to say, that they were in no way involved." I tapped my cheek with my finger. "Stripped? Only able to recover a tire or two? Blown up? Returned in pieces? Your subcontractor dead?"

Fab banged a spoon on the table. "You're not funny."

"I don't know about that — look around the table."

Fab shot glares at Didier and Creole, who were clearly entertained.

"My contractor and his friend ferreted out the location of the sports car, got it loaded on a flatbed, and were about to take off when gunshots rang out. Not just warning ones either. While returning fire, they called the cops. Law enforcement arrived in record time and got the situation under control."

"Is this the good part, where you tell us that everyone went to jail?" I tried to control my sarcasm and failed.

"If you didn't interrupt, I'd be finished by now."

I zipped my lips.

"Brick's three 'relatives' were booked on various gun charges. My guy produced legit paperwork, and he and his associate were released. He had another thing going for him—he's got several friends on the force that know him to be a straight arrow."

"I don't get why Brick is mad." Didier appeared puzzled. "Because the relatives are in jail?"

"Anyone want to put cash on there not being a DNA match between them? This is another job he'd say anything to get done." I wanted to strangle Brick. One of the reasons I loathed the man was he never thought about anyone but himself and what he wanted.

"Brick's livid that the cops showed up at his home in the early hours and hauled him in for questioning," Fab said. "It seems, when they searched the house in the Alley, they found a cache of guns and cash."

"Why were they interested in him if he was the victim?" Creole asked.

I'd never heard Brick described that way and almost laughed at the absurdity.

"One of the relatives, thinking to lessen his legal troubles, ratted on Brick, giving details on his cash car business. Mostly fabricated, according to Brick. On Brick's way out the door, he had his wife call his lawyer, who met them at the station. He claims he answered all their questions and was released. When I asked if he'd been warned not to leave town, he hung on me." Fab winced at the memory.

"Not very smart criminals. They had to know they wouldn't get away with stealing a Ferrari. Since they were up to their necks in illegal activities, they should've left the car alone," Creole said in disgust. "And to think they thought murdering two men was a better idea."

"The rest of the story?" I asked, knowing Brick's family members screwed one another on a regular basis, but not murder. Not in the past anyway.

"Brick's mistake was ignoring his own mandate and renting cars for cash again. These idiots figured that Brick had an illegal side business going and would never involve law enforcement. And as we both know, he never does. He's furious and blaming me, saying I should've told my guys no cops."

"Prick," I said.

"Madison," Creole admonished, then did a double-take. "Did I just morph into Didier on the language thing? What I should've said is that I can think of a few harsher words to describe the man."

I covered his hand with mine and squeezed.

"Let me get this straight—Brick thinks anyone you send on a job should risk their lives for a few bucks?" I asked. "You and I know that if we had done the job, those morons would be dead. And then so would Brick, because he'd disappear, never to be found."

Fab hung her head and rubbed her temples.

"What does Brick want?" Didier growled. "Since this is case closed as far as you're concerned."

"To let me know he's not paying."

"Oh yes he is," I seethed. "I volunteer to make the collection call myself. With a little hint about all the personal dirt I've been privy to over the years and wouldn't be the least bit hesitant to dig up and make public."

"Refusing to pay?" Creole cracked his knuckles. "Didier and I will pay him an office visit. It's been a while since I've blacked his eye; I'd enjoy doing it again. Maybe both this time."

"Admit it," I teased Fab. "Telling us all about it wasn't that painful."

Didier pulled Fab sideways into an awkward hug.

"Good thing I brought the kid or I wouldn't be able to get in," Brad announced from the patio doors, Liam by his side. "What, my key get lost in the mail?"

Liam waved.

"Security is Fab's domain." I came close to smiling at smoothly shuffling the problem into Fab's lap.

Didier stood, crossing into the outside kitchen, where he grabbed plates, handing one to Liam and pointing him to the barbeque.

"Key's in the mail," Fab said.

"Strangers don't get keys. Not sure you're my brother. Where's the designer suit?" I eyed his shorts and shirt—they had "upscale men's shop" written all over them but was still a departure from his usual uptight look. "Dude? Your image? You should've at least worn a tie."

Everyone laughed.

"Smells good." Brad sniffed. "Why don't I get invited for dinner anymore?"

Didier nudged him, pointing to a plate he'd set on the counter.

"You do. But you're always busy, with what I'm not sure—your excuses tend to be vague." I pointed to where Liam was piling food on his plate. "Help yourself. Then come sit and entertain us with stories about a day in the life of a soon-to-be real estate mogul."

Brad puffed out his chest and laughed. "It's probably too soon to put mogul on my business card."

Liam put his plate down, claiming a seat.

Creole took drink orders and refilled everyone's glasses. I covered mine, opting for water.

"How did you wrangle visitation from Mother?" I asked Brad.

To say she was possessive of Liam's time was an understatement, and that included time spent with either Brad or myself. Apparently, we all needed to be supervised. Brad took it in stride and was the only one to get her to back off and loosen up her controlling ways.

"I had to book in advance and warn her

several times that it was a guys' night out. I didn't actually say 'no women,' but she got the point," Brad said, and he and Liam shared a laugh.

"So, brother, what brings you by?" Fab asked. "In the neighborhood?"

"I know, I know, I've been scarce." He put his plate on the table and pulled two envelopes from his back pocket, handing one to Creole and the other to Didier.

Fab leaned over, peering at the envelope. "Didier plus one." She shot Brad a death stare.

I shook my head at Brad, glaring at him.

Creole looked down at the envelope and handed it to me. "I'll let my plus one open it. You're not getting us in trouble with your sense of humor. In case you've forgotten, Didier and I can take you."

"Admit it, I'm funny," Brad boasted.

I opened the envelope, took out the card, and started laughing. "My bro is having a Christmas party. Black tie."

"Tux?" Creole said incredulously. "And bowtie? Sorry, dude." He clapped Brad on the back. "We're busy that night."

"You'll have to change your plans—Mother is co-hosting. It started out a family affair, but when I ran my own party plans by her, she suggested that we combine the two. Dumping all the planning in her lap works for me. The woman knows how to throw a party." His dark eyes zeroed in on each of us in turn, finally landing on me. "If you can party at a funeral home, the least you can do is show up and act like you're having a good time."

"I'm RSVPing for all of us," Fab stated smugly. "We'll be there."

"You going?" I raised my eyebrow at Liam.

He nodded. "I'm working on a date. The girls I know at school left the state for break. Going to ask someone local."

"If you're looking for someone old enough to be your grandmother, I could probably introduce you," I offered.

"You know," he laughed, "that would be fun, just to see the reactions."

"I'm a bad influence."

"Not as much as I wish you were. You asked what I want for Christmas – lockpicking lessons."

"I knew this day was coming, and it's here," I groaned. "Nothing says 'holiday spirit' like lockpicking."

Fab slammed her hand on the table. "That was my gift idea."

I winked at Liam.

"What's for dessert?" he asked.

Chapter Ten

Fab had been driving me crazy, trying to come up with a holiday surprise for Didier. I'd thrown out my best ideas, most of which she sniffed at. Now when she brought up the subject, which was often, I ignored her. Finally, she decided on one of my ideas that met her standards.

First on her list was kicking Creole and me out of the house with the admonition to not come back until noon the following day. Creole was only too happy to comply, as lately we hadn't spent much time at his beach house, which was quieter than my house, with no unexpected guests stopping by.

Fab planned dinner for two—take-out, I assumed, since I'd never seen her even pick up a pot the whole time I'd known her—and we'd driven to a party store in Miami that came recommended by someone she knew. After trying on several outfits, she'd chosen a strapless red velvet Santa's helper costume, with white faux fur trim and a black belt, that cinched her waist and barely covered her silk-clad behind. I'd found the white, thigh-high stockings with bows, and the saleswoman had recommended boots.

"Didier prefers stilettos," Fab said in a breathy tone.

To my credit, I didn't roll my eyes.

The day had come, and I was happy to get out of the house. Fab had worked herself into a state, worrying over every little detail. I'd thought that was my job, but she was being more meticulous than I'd ever seen her.

I'd made plans of my own, but nothing as elaborate as Fab's. It was a beautiful day for a drive down the Overseas—blue skies, the sun glimmering off the water. Taking the turn-off to the beach house and rounding the curve, I was a bit disappointed that Creole's truck wasn't in the driveway. I slipped the picnic hamper, which I had filled to the brim with food for dinner, over one arm, tucked a blanket under the same arm, and with my free hand, reached for a foot-tall potted sago palm.

I managed to get everything inside with no mishaps, setting it all on the counter. Not sure how long I'd have to wait, I unpacked the food into the refrigerator. From the wine rack, I chose a bottle of Cabernet, setting it next to the basket.

The palm tree was my attempt to make up for the lack of holiday decorations. Reaching into my purse, I pulled out several strands of colored electric lights and draped the palm, making it the centerpiece on the coffee table. It looked a bit garish, but I liked it. After the New Year, I'd take it home, replant it into a larger pot, and find it a permanent place outside.

I crossed the living room to the patio doors and slid them open, welcoming in the salty sea air. When Creole remodeled, he'd gutted the small house and turned it into one large, open, airy space. Sliding around the bamboo screen and into the bedroom, I opened a drawer, taking out a black two-piece bathing suit and matching sheer, knee-length dress. I'd be ready for the beach by the time Creole got home.

The kitchen door clicked closed. Creole poked his head around the corner, and I asked, "How was your day, honey?"

"Busy," he said grumpily. A large shopping bag in his hand, he disappeared into the walk-in closet and came out empty-handed.

Waiting for him, I wrapped my arms around him, running my fingers up his back. Leaning back, I said, "Change into your bathing suit. I've got everything ready for a picnic on the beach."

"Sounds good." He kissed me hard.

I went into the kitchen to arrange the food inside the antique hamper that I'd scored from Junker's. The lidded wicker basket had caught my attention when he unloaded it off his truck. If I had hesitated, I'm sure he would've sold it in a heartbeat. I'd given it a good washing and replaced the plastic dinnerware and utensils with pottery dishes, real silverware, and linen napkins.

Creole would be happy—I'd gone to the fish

market and scored one of his favorite foods: salmon patties. I was just happy they came precooked. I'd chosen pasta and vegetable sides and stopped at the bakery for his favorite cheese rolls. I'd assembled the salmon burgers ahead of time, making everything easy. The last thing to go in the hamper was the bottle of wine.

Creole came into the kitchen in bathing trunks and a t-shirt, beach towels in hand. I handed him the hamper and grabbed the blanket I'd found in the linen closet at home right after I moved in; I knew I'd have a use for it one day. He led the way out to the patio, and I grabbed a large lantern, which he took from me, motioning for me to go ahead down the steps to the beach.

I led him to a spot not far from shore and smoothed out the blanket. Creole set the basket down, opened the lid, and removed the bottle of wine and two glasses. We sat side by side, enjoying the view of the water. The sea was calm tonight, not a single boat on the horizon.

"Eating outside never gets old." Creole popped the cork. "We're not going to have much time before the sun sets. If I'd known you had something special planned, I'd have been home sooner." He leaned down, brushing my lips with his.

"Well…" I tugged on his t-shirt. "I guess we'll just fumble around in the dark."

He handed me a glass and clinked it with his. "I like this—it's quiet, just the two of us."

I rested my forehead against his. "I plan to enjoy every minute of your undivided attention."

We sat with our hands entwined, watching the small waves lap the shore.

"The chief called today." He paused, seemingly lost in thought. "Told me that medical leave couldn't go on forever and asked when I would be back on the job."

"And you said?"

"Told him my doc said first of the year. He had the nerve to ask if I'd even seen a doctor."

"Not so nervy, since you haven't seen one recently." That had been a bone of contention between the two of us, but now didn't seem the right time to remind him.

"The chief threatened to call the doctor himself, check out my story. I called his bluff, told him to go ahead. I'm counting on doctor-patient confidentiality and his not finding out that I haven't been the most cooperative patient."

"You're probably safe there. I assume we're talking about Dr. A?" At his nod, I said, "He has experience with flaky patients; he won't rat you out. But he might use it to get you to come in for a check-up." I hoped it turned out that way. Blackmailing Creole to get him to take care of his health didn't bother me in the least.

"What's for dinner?" He fingered the lid of the hamper.

I slapped my hand down on the lid. "That's how you left it – a vague return date of January?"

He nodded. "The chief knows I'm struggling with what to do next, and he backed off, not wanting to push me into saying anything other than that I'll be back."

I removed his hand from the lid, opening it. "Dinner's a few of your favorites—one in particular: salmon burgers." I took out the plates, setting them on the blanket, then removed the food and laid it out. I playfully slapped his hand away, wanting to serve him.

After I handed him a plate, he removed the bun and sniffed.

I laughed. "That was so Fab of you."

"Smells good." He grinned. "What kind of surprise does Fab have for Didier? It's been a well-kept secret. If he knew, he would've said something, and he didn't."

I told him about the costume in exacting detail, sticking out my leg and mimicking putting on the bow-tie stockings that had caught my interest. "Dinner and jungle sex."

Creole roared with laughter. "You might want to think about borrowing that outfit one of these nights."

"Fab's not a sharer. And as I recall, you once told me the fewer clothes the better."

"I really should stop to think about the endless possibilities before blurting out my favorite no-clothes edict."

I lay back and laughed.

Chapter Eleven

"That was totally phony," I said to Fab, who'd yawned for the fifth time in the short ride from the house to The Cottages. "You just want me to ask about last night so you can brag about your romantic antics. Not going to do it." I stuck my fingers in my ears.

"You're a prude."

I wiped a non-existent tear from my cheek.

"Madeline called before you got home and wanted the details. She's going to buy her own costume."

Creole had driven me home that morning. He and Didier had made plans to go for a bike ride south to Marathon and left soon after.

"La, la, la." I turned to the passenger window, staring at the other cars. "Don't want to hear about what you and Mother talked about."

Fab turned into the driveway of The Cottages, snapping up the "office only" parking space. "This isn't going to take all day, is it?"

"Since you're so tired, why don't you take a nap in the office? If anything exciting happens, I'll call you."

"You're the one who needs a nap—you're so mean today."

I sniffed before she got out and shoved the door closed.

Fab whirled around, giving the property a slow scan. "I haven't seen the lights on at night yet. How do they look?"

"Like two drunks got together and challenged each other to a duel of decorating skills."

Fab struggled not to laugh, but did anyway. "Turned off, they look good."

"Gee, thanks."

Kevin caught my attention. It was clearly his day off, as he was dressed in bathing trunks and busy spraying down a surfboard with a hose at the opposite end of the driveway.

"Do we have to talk to him?" Fab nagged as I started in his direction.

I ignored her and kept walking.

"Nice board. You get tired of it, I'll take it for yard deco," I said. "I'm surprised no one's stolen it."

"I'd make sure they never got out of jail." He turned off the water and rolled up the hose. So he wasn't the one that threw it in the bushes when done.

"Speaking of… arrested anyone lately? You don't have to run down the entire list, I'm only interested in the people I know."

He leaned the board up against the side of his cottage. "It's been quiet lately, just the usual drunk and disorderly issues. Another bank got robbed. From the description this time, the weapon being used is actually a squirt gun. Know anything about it?"

"Squirt gun? Sounds dangerous, you better be careful." I looked over my shoulder at Crum's cottage. The bathroom window was closed, which meant he wasn't home. It hadn't taken him long to figure out it was the best place for eavesdropping on conversations going on in the driveway. "Where's Crum?"

"He's around somewhere. I've seen him at least a half-dozen times this morning. I'm his alibi if a heist took place earlier today. Let's hope some nimrod doesn't think the robberies are a great idea and we get a copycat."

Fab had ditched me and gone into the office; she was now headed my way with Mac in tow, decked out in a sleeveless red knit shift, a pile of Christmas tree necklaces around her neck.

"Miss your mall job?" I asked.

"Oh heck no." She didn't make eye contact, too busy fiddling with one of the necklaces that had stopped flashing on and off. "I heard that a few of Crum's groupies showed up and pitched tantrums that he'd gotten the boot." She got the necklace to light up again and held it up to her chest.

Kevin watched with a smirk, enjoying the show.

"Happy to be back. I don't have to stand all

day, and who knew that herding old people is harder than children." Mac winked at Kevin, who she'd caught leering at her. "Any problems while I was gone?" She didn't wait for an answer, knowing there hadn't been any. "No one moved, so that means you didn't put Fab in charge."

I didn't turn to catch Fab's reaction. Kevin was thoroughly entertained.

"There's one thing you're forgetting." Fab elbowed Mac.

"We're having a party." Mac elbowed Fab back, but only got air; the woman was smart enough to step back. "Fab told me that it's the same night as your family shindig." She whipped some folded envelopes out of her bra, handing one to me and one to Fab. "It would be helpful if you'd both participate in the gift exchange – attending or not."

Fab scowled at her.

"I know Miss Prissy thought she wouldn't be putting out, but she's wrong," Mac said. Hands on her hips, chest thrust out, she turned to Fab. "You going to blow off my request? I need to know. Before answering, remember all the nice things I've done for you and also factor in holiday spirit."

Kevin's laughter didn't go unnoticed.

Before Fab could serve up a snarky retort, I said, "We'll be happy too, won't we, Prissy?"

Fab shot me a look of pure disgust and shoved

the envelope in the pocket of her jeans.

"And you." Mac whirled on Kevin. "Here's yours." She pulled out another envelope, making a person wonder how much room she had in her bra, all things considered. "Not one word of complaint out of you either."

Kevin turned on the boyish charm that he reserved for non-work days. "I'll give you the money. You buy something, wrap it, scribble my name on whatever it is, and let me know what I bought."

"Men," Mac grumbled. "Don't go all hog-wild; the budget's ten bucks."

Ten? I had no clue what I'd buy, but I'd figure that out once I found out whose name I got. Maybe I'd get lucky and be able to just put a bow on a twelve-pack. "I'll stop by the night of the party to say hello and drop off gifts."

Chapter Twelve

At my request and with some grumbling, Fab detoured to the bank on the way home. We rarely went inside, opting to do everything online, but this was one of those times I needed to drop off paperwork for the bank manager.

"We should've made this our first stop. Now we'll probably have to wait," Fab said, drumming her fingers against the steering wheel. Traffic was annoying her more than usual today, in part due to a road construction slowdown. At the first opening, she zipped around an old Impala, opting not to scare the man at the wheel by coming within an inch of his bumper.

"That's a bad time—the robberies have been happening right when the banks open. You never know which location is going to be next."

Her headshake conveyed that she thought I was out of my mind. She turned into the parking lot and took the space the armored truck had just vacated.

"At least we know they have plenty of cash," I said.

Before getting out of the car, Fab reminded me, "I told you I'd only come to the bank with you if you speed it along and don't dawdle."

"You can sit in the car if you promise to behave yourself and pinkie swear to be here when I come out." I stuck out my little finger, which she ignored.

"Forget that." She got out. "You need me to prod you along so you don't get all caught up in those folksy stories you like to listen to."

The two of us walked across the sidewalk and into the bank. Almost as soon as we'd signed in and claimed two chairs in the waiting area, a weird sound from the front of the teller line had us looking in unison at what was happening. A piercing scream ripped through the air, echoing in our ears.

Of the two tellers who worked the counter, one's face had gone ghostly white. Eyes bugged out, she turned toward her co-worker at the other end of the counter. Their hands shot into the air at the same moment. The other teller was also pale, her eyes focused on the man who proudly stood at the front of the line, gun in hand, amused at how he'd grabbed everyone's attention.

He was tall, with dark hair that was partially exposed under the fake combination white wig and beard that sat haphazardly on his head, some kind of goo on his face distorting the rest of his features. Red knee-length trunks, a tropical shirt, and a white plastic lei completed his outfit. His eyes stabbed the handful of people in the bank—eight, including the employees—silently daring them to do something, even though no one said a word after the scream. We were all completely paralyzed, a dead silence filling the space.

Until Fab leaned in and whispered, "Flip you for which one of us gets to shoot him."

"That's a real gun," I pointed out the obvious. Thanks to my brother, I'd had a good education in identifying handguns, and Santa was packing a Ruger .38 Special. The bank robber the cops were looking for had used a squirt gun in his most recent heist. Which one was the original and which was the copycat? "Let's see where this goes. I've never been to a bank robbery before."

"This isn't a party." In a deep voice, he instructed everyone except one teller to gather in the waiting area. He talked to us as though we were invited guests, keeping our attention with his commands, even though that wasn't necessary, since the Ruger was ready to shoot anyone who disobeyed his orders.

I studied the man behind the ratty beard, who appeared barely out of puberty, early twenties maybe. Another thing that stood out was that he spoke as though he'd been well educated. It irked me that he'd decided to besmirch Santa Claus, one of my favorites, by wearing his less-than-dramatic and unoriginal outfit while committing a felony. While the situation was dangerous and definitely stupid, it wouldn't take much for it to get out of hand and result in someone ending up dead. I stayed silent while "Santa" continued his monologue.

"I'd appreciate it if everyone stayed calm," the man said. "Make my job easier, and as a gift for being good, you get to live."

I was happy the man didn't hear Fab's snort.

"As you're finding out, I'm here to take something from you, and you're going to let me do it."

His voice was incredibly calm; he didn't appear worried about the police or anything else. With all the attention the robberies had generated, including the description of his so-called costume, I wondered why no one had noticed the man the second he stepped into the lobby.

"Jewelry, money, whatever you have of value." He waved his gun in the direction of the teller. "Get moving and fill up that bag," he said to her. "One minute. That's how long I'm willing to wait. If you fail… I wouldn't want to be you. Trust me. Come on now, give me what I politely asked for." His tone had turned sarcastic.

"Over your dead body," Fab whispered.

The woman across from us whimpered. "You're a monster."

Santa didn't take kindly to that comment. After a few seconds of silence, he raised the gun without a word and pointed it at the woman. She hid her face in her hands and started to cry.

"I'm pretty sure that we can shoot him without ending up in jail ourselves," I said, just loud enough for Fab to hear.

"If he demands something from one of us, we're going to find out."

"We also have to make certain he doesn't shoot anyone else."

Fab knew as well as I did that we couldn't reach for our handguns without tipping him off. Today, we both had them holstered at the smalls of our backs.

"Silence. All I ask for is quiet and that you do what you're told. Next time, it will be your head," he said, his smiling expression replaced with a bored one.

I moved my hand along the side of the chair, poking the phone in Fab's back pocket and snapping my fingers, hand out. I didn't see a way to reach into my bra and take mine out without anyone noticing.

Fab handed me hers, holding out three fingers.

I put it between my legs and pushed speed dial. As soon as the call connected, I said in a whiny voice, "Sorry for speaking, but couldn't you just rob the bank and let us go?" It surprised me to learn that, in addition to helping himself to the bank's money, he robbed the customers. That tidbit had never come out in any news article.

The Santa wannabe took his focus off the teller packing the money in the bag and turned it on Fab and I, putting a finger to his lips. "I'm in charge. My plan." He returned his attention to the teller.

"Creole?" Scanning every corner of the bank, Fab nodded at the phone, murmuring, "That trick worked once before; hopefully, it will this time. Creole's not stupid."

I nodded and looked around, trying to come up a contingency plan fast.

Santa stood watch, seemingly confidant, waiting for one of the women across from him and the man to take out their valuables. I was certain that this wasn't the first time he'd done something like this, copycat or not. I was also sure that this would be his last. A little patience, and this would finish as it should, with him in custody. His eyes darted around, making eye contact with everyone, scanning the space as he checked out the only other man and dismissed him, not seeing the older man as a threat. Why would he? There were only a few people there to scare, and he did that right off. Everyone had heeded his threats and done everything they were told, and it was doubtful that they'd do anything crazy to try to stop him.

Santa began collecting jewelry and watches, even cash, everything people turned over, and all with a smile on his face.

"Once I've finished up here, your lives can go back to normal and I'll be richer. Fair, don't you think? You're all behaving and should be able to say goodbye to each other without incident."

Oddly, his voice didn't seem as confident as before. I'd noticed that he checked one of the watches before pocketing it. Why the change? Could it be he had allotted a certain amount of time to get in and out and he'd surpassed it? Santa came to stand in front of me.

I held out my palms. "Sorry, I don't have any valuables. Only brought in this pile of paperwork." I motioned to the chair next to me.

His finger shifted on the trigger. My heart racing, I flinched involuntarily, and it took a moment for me to realize I'd just heard a distinctive click. "Santa" looked momentarily disconcerted. Through my fading panic, I realized that he'd just slipped and given himself away, and no one had noticed except Fab and me. We exchanged a secretive smile. That click had meant one of two things: either the gun misfired or he didn't have any bullets. Possibly he'd failed to load his weapon, or maybe he didn't have any ammunition to begin with. Maybe he thought if he brandished an unloaded firearm, if caught, he wouldn't get the automatic additional ten-year sentence. I mulled over my ridiculous idea, but then, maybe it wasn't. Why not? People had been immobilized by one look at the gun pointed in their direction and his confidant attitude. Advantage Fab and me—we had two working firearms.

He shot me a disgusted look and moved to Fab. "I tagged along with her." She pointed at me. "My purse is in the car if you'd like me to go get it."

They engaged in a stare-down.

He muttered, moving on to the bank manager.

I tried to catch the attention of the people across from me and signal them to get Santa to turn around. The two that made eye contact stared back as though I was certifiable and no reply was necessary. They weren't in on the plan and weren't willing to take any risks. I could hardly blame them; they didn't know me, and even if they had, their reaction might still have been the same.

The tension ratcheted up when the man across from me put a hand to his throat, wheezing, trying to catch a breath.

Santa turned his head, and while he was attempting to control the situation, Fab pulled her weapon, keeping it hidden for the moment. The only problem was that Santa was standing too close to the man for her to get a clean shot.

"I'll shoot you!" Santa shouted at the man. But his threat wasn't followed by a bullet, which made me more certain of my theory that he wasn't armed.

"I've… got asthma…" the man tried to say while his breathing gradually got harder and harder.

"I don't care. When you're dead, you won't have to worry about your asthma," Santa said, drops of sweat rolling down from under his beard, dripping on his shirt.

"He'll die if you don't let him use his meds," I said loudly, "ensuring you get the death penalty when you're caught."

The woman next to him, her face filled with worry and eyes brimming with tears, started crying again. The manager's face burned with anger, her hands clenched at her side.

I jumped up, having decided to be the distraction and hope this didn't backfire, so I could listen to one of Creole's lengthy lectures on personal safety. "Santa's out of bullets," I announced. "He's not much of a threat."

"Liar!" Santa pointed his gun directly at me.

"Drop it," Fab said, and a second later, shot him in the shoulder.

I'd ducked, and when I glanced up, I was surprised to see that Fab hadn't put the bullet between his eyes. Maybe I was rubbing off on her – a little, anyway.

Santa dropped the gun, grabbing his arm, and ran towards the door.

"I've called the cops; they'll be here any second," I yelled. In fact, just then, several police cars blew into the parking lot.

Santa apparently didn't notice and ran out the door into the raised weapons of the local cops, which had him skidding to a stop, his good hand shooting into the air, he turned slightly, his expression a mixture of surprise and anger. They ordered him to the ground, and he obeyed.

"That was brave of you," Fab said. "Regardless of what we suspected about whether he had more bullets or not."

"A little improv was needed. The last thing I wanted was for that other man to die because we didn't do anything."

Fab nudged me. "Our security detail just showed up."

I followed her gaze to where Creole leaned against the back of his truck, Didier beside him. They both had their arms crossed. "We need to remind those two that it's not like we left the house this morning thinking we'd go to a bank robbery."

"I'll be your backup on this one."

"You're the best."

"Don't—"

Before she could get the words out, I hugged her anyway.

Chapter Thirteen

Two parties the same day — who does that? I asked myself again. The season was now racing to a close, and tonight would be the end of the parties. The last few days before Christmas were going to be relaxing because I planned to decree just that in the morning. The shopping was done, the packages wrapped and stuffed under the tree.

The Cottages' holiday bash had undergone a few alterations after the invitations were received and the partygoers complained that it was too fancy. Always willing to improvise, Mac listened to the grievances, and the evening party morphed into a late-afternoon barbeque by the pool so those that needed to be in bed by eight wouldn't miss anything.

The latest plan made it easy for me to put in an appearance and then get back home and change for the second party of the evening.

I pulled on a red, knee-length tiered cotton skirt I'd found while shopping with Fab, paired it with a white short-sleeved t-shirt, and slipped my feet into shell-trimmed red flip-flops. I grabbed my purse and headed for the stairs.

Creole looked up, stood, and met me at the bottom.

"Your date awaits you." He stuck out his arm.

"You're going?" I eyed him suspiciously.

It annoyed me to no end that Fab was leading the whiner parade, lying on the couch with Didier's arms around her. Both had refused to put in an appearance at The Cottages party with me. Creole didn't want to attend either, but *he* hadn't outright refused. Both men had lit out earlier, dragging their feet somewhere with vague excuses about errands, and it surprised me that they were now back.

"I can't let my favorite girl party without me." Creole gave me a cheeky grin.

Fab made a sick noise, sounding like the cat horking up a hairball. I groaned inwardly. Wait until she got that noise perfected—I'd hear it non-stop until she got bored.

"Good one." Didier gave him a thumbs up and laughed at the glare he got in return.

I checked Creole over from head to toe. He was in linen shorts, his t-shirt hugging his abs. "You'll need to change. A sweater and jeans would be good."

Fab growled. "If Didier were going, you'd suggest he strip to a pair of speedos. Eye candy was the word you used once."

Creole and Didier laughed.

"Is this where I say sorry?" I stuck out my lower lip.

"Don't forget my gift." Fab pointed to what looked suspiciously like a liquor bottle factory-wrapped in a holiday-themed box.

It annoyed me that she wouldn't tell me whose name she'd gotten. I got one of our female Canadian guests—she and her husband were here for the season, which lasted from November to April. To say it was hard to choose something for someone I'd only shared a few words with would be an understatement. I opted for chocolates from a family-owned store in Marathon. They'd not only wrapped the box but put it in a small shopping bag for a great presentation.

Creole picked up her gift and mine, grabbed my hand, and we headed out the door.

Creole rounded the corner to The Cottages, and I directed him to park at Mac's. She'd said that way I didn't run the risk of getting blocked in and having to run down the driver of the offending car.

He cut off the engine, then leaned over and kissed me. "Any tips on how to handle this crowd?"

"If in doubt as to what to say, smile, then change the subject. You can't do that too many times, though, or Crum will spread the rumor that you're stupid."

"Dare him to say it to my face."

I laughed.

Creole got out and went around, opening the passenger door, lifting me into his arms, and setting me on the ground. We walked across the street, where Mac saw us coming and met us halfway.

"We've got beer and cold drinks at the bar. No wine drinkers in this crowd." She led us to the pool area, directing Creole to where he could put the gifts.

The gate had been propped open, and several of the guests lying on the chaises waved and shouted hello. I waved back and so did Creole.

"You've already attracted the attention of the ladies," I said.

"You're going to protect me, aren't you?"

"No worries there. I'll go all cavegirl and scare them." He laughed. "Then they'll go back to their home country and tell their friends I'm bat crazy, and the reservations will fly in."

Having overheard, Mac said, "We stay booked year round. They come for entertainment and I deliver. No more planned fights," she reassured Creole, who'd told her to stop them before someone got hurt. "But when one breaks out spontaneously, it helps."

"There's Joseph and his, uhm…" Creole nodded toward the man in question.

"Svetlana," I reminded him. I turned to say hello to Joseph, kissing his blow-up girlfriend on the cheek. "She's looking fabulous," I told Joseph, who had dressed her in a red dress with a slit up the thigh, showing a tanned leg. "You doing okay? I heard you quit your elf job."

"I tried it for a few days with the replacements, and it wasn't a stick of fun. The ladies stopped coming around. All my co-workers did was complain about sore feet and…" He paused, looking at Creole. "…other stuff. Not having the guts to quit, I came to work drunk. That worked." He hacked out a laugh.

"You mind if I touch?" Creole asked, indicating Svetlana. "I haven't seen one up close."

Joseph shoved Svetlana into his arms. "I've got to run into the house. Don't take your eyes off her. She's been kidnapped a couple of times."

I nodded with open amusement, letting him know nothing would happen in his absence.

"She's so lifelike, it's a little creepy," Creole said.

"Svet's my favorite tenant. Like Kitty, Miss January's long-deceased cat, she has a permanent home here. You're lucky Fab's a no-show. She'd already have her camera out and a handful of pictures of you and the beautiful blonde taken to blackmail you with."

"I'd sic you on her."

Mac returned with Joseph. "Everyone wants to say hello to you. You're the star, as they only get glimpses of you from time to time."

"You want me to mingle and do small talk? I'm so bad at it."

Mac snorted. "This from the woman who can talk to anyone. Leave the boyfriend here; I'll entertain him." She smiled at Creole.

He shook his finger at her. "You're a troublemaker."

"Only sometimes." She smirked.

Miss January stumbled through the gate. It was late for her to be out and about. Normally, she'd be passed out by this time of day, sleeping off her all-day drunk.

"Keep an eye on her," I told Mac. "I don't want her falling in the pool."

"Hi, hon." Miss January patted Svetlana on the arm. Joseph had taken her back and sat her in a chair next to him.

"Where's your new beau?" I asked, looking out into the driveway.

"He's not a people person." She cackled and pulled a flask out of her pocket, unscrewing the lid and taking a long swig. "Sure miss having you as a neighbor." She winked at Creole.

That was so long ago, I was surprised she remembered.

"Congratulations on the new relationship. He better treat you right." Creole flexed his muscles, which had her giggling.

Crum stuck his head out his bathroom window, peered around, and disappeared, shutting the window.

"Why isn't Mr. Life of the Party out here?" I asked Mac.

Joseph answered. "He's embarrassed that people know he got hauled in for questioning in the bank heists."

"Someone needs to have a talk with him." I stared at Mac. "Point out that it has the potential to enhance his bad-boy image."

"You tell him. He never listens to me."

Just then, Kevin walked through the gate. "Food and beer. My kind of party." He tipped his bottle at us.

"What's the latest on the bank robber case?" Creole asked.

Kevin laughed in disgust. "Turns out Santa was a bored twenty-something. James Howell the fifteenth or some such BS. Made sure we knew his family's stinkin' rich. Good thing for him, since they had to post a hefty cash bail. He exercised his right to remain silent, not saying a word until his high-priced attorneys showed up, all three of them."

"I'd say the case is a slam dunk," Creole said. "He was, after all, caught running out of the bank, leaving behind a gun with his prints on it and a handful of eye witnesses. He'll be doing prison time."

"Howell doesn't seem to think so. Got an attitude that he can do whatever he wants; boasted he's got enough money to buy himself out of trouble."

"Bored rich kid?" I asked. "His answer was to rob a bank?"

"Pretty much." Kevin downed his beer, passing the bottle off to Mac with a wink. "Happy it's not my case. According to the arresting officers, he was a whiney pain on the way to the hospital and didn't shut his mouth until they put him under anesthesia to fix that shoulder."

Creole tapped his watch. "We need to leave if we're going to get to your mother's party on time."

"Give me a couple of minutes." I grabbed Mac's arm, and we made the rounds. Although I'd waved whenever someone new came through the gate, I knew they wanted something friendlier. I thanked everyone for coming and let them know I'd be around more after the first of year and that Mac was the queen of problem-solving.

It took more time than I expected. Every time I looked over my shoulder, the group of men laughing and joking near the bar had grown larger. Seeing Creole at the center had me smiling.

"Your party is a wild success," I congratulated Mac.

All the tenants and their guests were caught up in spirited conversations around the pool. Not a single person was left out. Mac led me over to the table and handed me two gifts that she had sitting in a chair. Then she wrapped her arms around me in a bear hug.

"This was fun," I squeaked.

Chapter Fourteen

"I don't want to go," Creole whined, jerking on the knot of his tie until it didn't choke him any longer. At least, I assumed so, since he stopped complaining and making sound effects.

He'd come close to braking for every green light on the way home from The Cottages, until I reminded him that the only thing worse than being late was calling with a last-minute excuse.

"Hot." I made a sizzling sound, my eyes sweeping over his black suit.

He'd refused to go rent a tux, which it turned out he didn't have to since the whole black-tie idea had been a joke my brother thought would be funny to pull on his friends. Didier had been the one to find out after bringing up the subject with Mother.

"Didn't Brad tell you? That's his idea of a joke," Mother had said.

"It's funny all right," Didier had said sarcastically.

Spoon had added to the drama by threatening to wear an ugly sweater, which he said was better than any "damn monkey suit."

"Your decision," I said. "We can be the one

couple that bails, but the catch is you have to be the one to make the excuses. I'm telling you now, it better be a doozy, something along the lines of you got a call from one of your law enforcement friends and he tipped you off the end of the world is happening tonight." That made him laugh and his frown disappear.

"I'll need some incentive." He checked me out from head to toe.

I twirled around in my red silk, short-sleeved, above-the-knee sheath dress, which got Fab's approval in the store as soon as I held it up. She'd bought something similar, only in black and sleeveless.

"If—" I shook my finger at him, and he nibbled on the end. "—you're really good, you can peek under my dress later."

"I want to do it now," he said with a wolfish smile.

"So sorry." I gave him a pouty frown. "Fab and Didier are waiting. And we wouldn't want to be late." I grabbed his hand and tugged him into the hall.

"Ta da," I said as we descended the stairs.

"Très belle," Didier said to me, and I smiled back. "I'm surprised you didn't rebel and wear bathing trunks." He laughed at Creole.

"I could change." He looked at me hopefully. "My red trunks, no shirt, and a black leather tie."

"I want to dare you…" I laughed. "…but I'm afraid you'll do it."

"Let's get this party on the road," Didier said.

"We're already going to be late." Fab headed for the door. "You know your mother hates that, and then we'll have to hear about it for a week."

The entrance to the Key Resort was beautiful at night, palm trees wrapped in lights running the length of the long driveway from the road to the lobby of the building. Creole waylaid one of the valets and got directions to the restaurant. Once there, the hostess led us out onto a pier that extended out over the Gulf. Lights were strung overhead, sparkling off the water, with Christmas trees every few feet, the largest one at the end where we were to be seated.

One long, oblong table had been set in red, white, and green linen, with silver and crystal, the red-and-green striped umbrellas overhead also draped in lights. Small square lanterns dotted the middle of the table, each holding a candle surrounded by seashells.

Mother and Spoon greeted us, and we exchanged kisses. Mother had chosen a knee-length green dress, and Spoon had worn a suit after all, no tie. She introduced us to four other couples I'd never met, explaining that they were business associates of Brad.

Frankly, I was impressed that she could keep the names straight. "Where is my brother?" I asked, looking around.

"Brad called to say he and Phil had just pulled into the parking lot. They should be here in a minute or two."

The back half of the deck had been cordoned off, with a full bar set up in front of a small sitting area of chairs and side tables that wrapped around a dance floor. All of Brad's friends had drifted toward the bar and were talking, drinks in hand. I recognized one non-family member that had me groaning inwardly, a business associate of Brad's that he'd recently partnered with on a local project.

What was Mother thinking? More than half the people at the table would be unknown to the other half. My brother and his lawyer/girlfriend, Philipa Grey aka Phil, would be the only ones his business associates knew.

Brad had yet to find out that I'd had a background check done on his girlfriend. It had come back clean. But something about the woman still nagged at me. Phil had bartended at Jake's for years while going to law school, and Fab and I had trusted her implicitly then, but the second she passed the bar, she'd morphed into a completely different person.

I leaned into Fab. "We need to search the table for place cards, snatch them up, and change the seating to our benefit. I'm not sitting next to a stranger all night, schmoozing for my brother."

"Already done." Fab smiled devilishly. "Don't

tell, but Didier and I worked the table as a team."

It wasn't the first time we'd pulled that trick. Until Mother caught one of us red-handed, it would continue. I had no doubt Fab could get herself out of trouble; as for myself, I'd need some help.

"Let's hope when it's time to make small talk, you remember all the names," Fab said. "I forgot already."

Creole laughed. He'd just come up, drinks in hand, and handed Fab a martini and me a glass of wine. "Me too. When your brother mentioned a couple of business associates, I thought he meant his new partner, not a whole crew of people."

"Whose idea was it to combine family and business?" Didier asked.

"Mother/Madeline," Fab and I said at the same time.

"My guess," I said, "is that Mother talked Brad into it, telling him what a great idea it would be. You know how she loves putting dinners together, and this way, she has the opportunity to check everyone out."

A woman at the opposite end of the pier began setting up her microphone and attracted some attention by performing a sound check. Curvy in a colorful Boho maxi dress split up the front, her dark curly hair hanging down her back, she settled on a stool under a spotlight. After some banter with the people sitting nearby, she picked up her guitar and unleashed her beautiful bluesy voice.

"Heads up," Creole said. "Liam's here with his... date."

I groaned. "What's Kevin done now?" I'd cringed when I heard he was fixing Liam up with a friend of a friend. "This girl is supposed to be a college student and only a couple years older than him."

Didier watched as the two talked to Mother and Spoon. "She's twenty?"

Peering around Creole's side, I could only see their backs. "Let's go meet her."

Didier took Fab's drink from her hand. Setting it down, he pulled her into his arms, and they made use of a small section of the dance floor.

Spoon waylaid Creole, asking him a question, and they got caught up in conversation, leaving me to go check out Liam's date.

"You look nice," I said to Liam.

Mother gave him a nod and a wink, showing her approval.

Liam had told me he asked Didier for help in picking out the black suit and they drove to Miami after making an appointment with one of Didier's connections.

"This is Becca," Liam introduced his date.

The twenty-year-old, if she was one, looked closer to thirty. Her body shape reminded me of Dolly Parton, and she had a head full of springy blond curls. Her short black dress hit her at mid-thigh and framed her curves, and she was wearing the highest stilettos I'd ever seen. Fab would have a case of shoe envy when she got a look at that pair.

"Nice to meet you," I said sincerely. "I hear you two met through Kevin."

"I got to know Kevin when he lived next door. My sister and he were briefly neighbors… until his building burned down. My sister had always commented on how safe she felt, having him so close," Becca said, making a good first impression.

"Happy to hear Kev's fulfilling his oath to protect and serve," whispered Creole, who'd just showed up at my side.

I nudged him.

The music ended, and Fab and Didier joined us. Liam made the introductions, and Fab immediately engaged Becca in a conversation about shoes. Creole and I moved to the banister, facing one another.

"Before dinner would be a good time for us to make the rounds and say, 'Nice to meet you. What's your name again?'" Creole suggested.

"Maybe." It was the last thing I wanted to do. I grinned up at him. "I'd rather stand here and gawk—messy hair, open shirt, the way your pants hug your hips."

He leered down at me. "What was I saying?"

"Not sure."

He brushed a kiss against my lips.

Brad cleared his throat, tapping a knife on the side of a glass, and motioned for everyone to find their place card and take a seat. Fab had arranged to have Mother, Spoon, Brad, his friends, and their dates at one end of the table, and the rest of us at the opposite end, next to the tree. From what I could see, everyone appeared to be relaxed and having a good time.

I whispered to Liam, "You're sitting down at this end with the fun people. Another plus: Creole and Didier won't be staring at your date like she's a delectable morsel like I caught a couple of the others doing."

"Becca's used to the attention, and it doesn't bother her one way or the other. She mostly ignores it. Because of her, I ignore it too. When we go out, our attention is on each other."

"I like her." I kissed his cheek. "You two having a good time is all I care about."

Mother glanced at several place cards, then straightened and shot me a glare. In return, I smiled at her, adding a subtle thumbs up, pretending I had no clue what was up.

Liam pulled out Becca's chair, and before he sat, Fab whispered her approval. He told the two of us, "This is our third date, and so far, we've had a lot of fun doing low-key things. I'm looking forward to hanging out with her during break."

Once everyone was seated, Brad, who had stayed standing, raised his glass in a toast and thanked everyone for coming.

As the servers cleared the plates, one came around and refilled drink glasses. Even though I wasn't driving, I waved off a refill, as did everyone at our end of the table.

The music came to a halt when four uniformed officers made their way down the deck. In true Keys style, all eyes were on the unfolding drama. No one moved, instead settling back in their seats for a ringside view. Creole had his back turned, and I lightly kicked him and motioned with my head.

"Look, Mommy," a small kid shrieked. "Cops."

The officers came to a stop surrounding a table where a young couple sat. The woman hung her head, and the man did all the talking. After an exchange, the woman kicked her chair back, knocking one officer in the knees, and in two steps, hurled herself over the deck railing, swan diving into the water.

Several nearby people flew out of their seats and over to the railing, phones out and aimed down at the water. All the overhead lighting twinkling off the inky water made it easy to see where she landed.

"She's swimming away," one man shouted.

One officer yelled for everyone to remain

seated as the others took off running.

The man the jumper had been with had waved when she made her leap. Now he moved to the railing and watched the drama below, a smirk on his face.

Fab and I looked at one another and rolled our eyes, both of us thinking, "not a good getaway plan."

"Dude set her up," Creole whispered, just loud enough for those at our end of the table to hear. "Looks pretty proud of himself."

"She's swimming over to the beach," a woman updated everyone.

Minutes later, the sound of speedboats could be heard approaching.

The man she was with fist-pumped and called out, "Got her!" He threw some cash on the table and started back up the pier.

Someone yelled, "Hey pal, what did she do?"

The man paused, appeared to be about to say something, then continued on his way instead.

"Hey man, it must be something good. Tell us," someone else yelled.

"Read about it online in the morning." He paused, then added, "Or wait for the weekly."

Brad broke the silence at the table. "Hey sis," he called from the other end of the table. "Friend of yours?"

His friends laughed.

Creole growled.

I laid my hand on Creole's arm. "I did

recognize her. Didn't you date her?" There were a couple of titters, most of them finding my brother funnier than me.

Brad saluted me with his glass. "Good one."

Fab glared down the table. "I dare him to ask *me* that."

Creole and Didier laughed.

"I haven't drunk enough to make a scene, but we could remedy that," I said to Fab.

The two of us exchanged smirks. It never got old, having a friend that always had your back.

"I think I'd enjoy that." Creole hugged me. "What about you, Didier?"

Chapter Fifteen

It was the last weekend before Christmas, and the four of us agreed we were partied out. We made plans to do nothing and spend an uneventful day hanging around the house. Since we'd eaten all the leftovers earlier, Creole offered to go pick something up for dinner if we could agree. My phone rattled across the island, intruding on the rustling of to-go menus. Four pairs of eyes flew to the screen. A picture of the exterior of Jake's popped up, and I slid it away from Fab's reaching fingers. "It's not your phone," I reminded her.

Creole and Didier, mimicking Fab's bad habit, didn't bother to hide their intention of listening in. Fab signaled for me to hit the speaker button, which I ignored.

"Anyone die?" I answered.

Fab drummed her fingers impatiently. Didier grinned.

Half-expecting Fab to grab my phone out of my fingers, I gave into that unspoken threat and the impatient eyes staring me down and hit the speaker button, setting it on the countertop.

"Hey boss, hate to bother you, but as you know, tonight is Santa night."

Creole rolled his eyes.

"Backup bartender got in a fender bender on the way here. He's all right but has to deal with his car. One of his front tires and wheel well took a pounding. I've got Mac to fill in, but she can't be here for a couple of hours. I hate to ask, but…"

"No worries. I'm the owner — who better to fill in?" I let out a small sigh. "Be there in fifteen." I made a face at Creole, who crossed his arms, a militant look on his face.

"Thanks, it's only until Mac gets here," Doodad assured me. "If we weren't so busy, I wouldn't have called."

"No problem."

We disconnected.

"You're not going," Creole grated through clenched teeth. "There have been more bar fights than usual since the start of these *theme* nights, some spilling out into the parking lot."

"They've been wildly popular," I countered. "Jake's is now almost one of the hottest places to grab a beer." I knew it wasn't what we served on tap but the sideshows that were drawing the crowds.

Fab smirked. I kicked her under the counter.

"Ouch." She glared.

"Name one of these events where there hasn't been trouble," Creole said, voice on the rise. "The only time the cops weren't involved, I was there to get your revelers under control." He added, "*You* could get hurt."

"It's only for a couple of hours. What could go wrong?"

"Make yourself comfortable while I run down a list for you."

"Are we fighting?" I frowned.

"We're discussing."

Fab laughed. Didier gave a poor imitation of a glare in response.

"I've got a plan." I came around the island, taking his hand in mine. "Since you don't have a Santa suit, all you'd need to do is change into something red."

"What? I'm your bodyguard?"

"Surprised you didn't think of it."

"I did, but I liked my plan to steal you away to the beach, just the two of us, better." He wagged his brows.

"Fab and I volunteer to come along," Didier offered.

Fab humphed.

"We've got this." I winked at her. Creole picked me up, throwing me over his shoulder, and carried me up the stairs.

Despite Creole's attempts to distract me from leaving the bedroom, we finally made it to Jake's—fifteen minutes later than I'd promised.

The parking lot was over half-full, which for us meant a busy night. I directed him to drive around the back of the building and park next to the kitchen door.

"Stop," I said, rolling down the window as he slowed going by Junker's. "Wow, where do you think he got that?" I pointed to an eight-foot statue.

Creole lowered his head, peering out the passenger window. "What the heck is it?"

"The most famous snowman of all." I laughed at his confusion. "Frosty."

"Looks to be constructed of cement. It's got to weigh a few hundred pounds." The headlights illuminated the statue, which needed a bath and a paint job.

"It reminds me of the lighthouse. It just needs a little TLC."

"You need to ask yourself how it got here. Stolen, possibly. Suspicious, just like the lighthouse."

"You're so negative. The cops have had plenty of time to impound the house, but no, there it sits." I waved. "They sometimes park their cruisers over there to catch speeders."

"Great, you've got yourself a speed trap on the property." He gunned the engine and squealed into the parking space at the back entrance. "I'm telling you now — you're not taking Frosty home. Santa wouldn't appreciate the competition, not to mention the fact that no one would be able to park in the driveway."

I powered up the window, smiling. "Oh, okay."

He got out and walked around to the passenger side, pulled me across the seat into his arms, and kissed me until all thoughts of Frosty were forgotten.

"I'm taking my guarding-your-body duty seriously tonight," he said sternly. "You will stay out of trouble."

"What fun is that?"

He scooped me in his arms and kissed me until my toes reached the ground. "If I have my way, you're in for a boring stint behind the bar."

"And just because you're looking all hot and sexy in those bathing trunks, there's a no-touching-by-other-women policy. Got it?"

He saluted. "Yes, ma'am." He twirled around. "You think I'm sexy?"

"I'd have to be unconscious not to think that."

Doodad, looking a bit harried, waved as we approached from the hallway. Traditional tropical Santas were knee-deep at the bar. Looking around the room, I saw that a few had donned only a hat and some hadn't bothered to get in the spirit at all. Doodad had wanted to ban those that didn't dress up, but since this was his idea, he didn't want to jinx the turnout. He needn't have worried—the place was packed, with music blaring from the jukebox, and even the deck was crowded.

I slid behind the bar, nodding to Doodad, who was refereeing while a couple of regulars tossed quarters into a shot glass.

Creole took up his post at the end of the bar in front of the garnish box and scanned for any faces that matched the wanted posters at the local post office. Last time I was in, there'd been one.

A robust fellow in red Santa pants, a wife beater, and black suspenders banged his beer bottle on the bar. "I'll have another," he slurred.

Thinking he needed to be cut off, I asked, "You got a ride home?"

Doodad had hired Jimbo, an off-duty cab driver, for free rides. Paid him a flat rate and let him keep all the tips. Must be lucrative because he was back shooting darts in the corner.

"Got my reindeer parked out front." The man snapped his suspenders, flinched, and scratched his chest. "Went out there a couple of times but couldn't find the bad boys. If someone took them, they have a serious ass-kicking coming."

"Don't worry." I set another bottle in front of him and glanced at Doodad, mouthing, *He needs a ride*. "Probably just a joyride. They'll be back and parked right where you left them in no time." Good sense kept me from turning in Creole's direction; if he'd overheard the conversation, he wouldn't be amused.

"Giddy up." The man grabbed his bottle and jumped toward the crowd. At the dance floor, he extended his arms and waltzed his way across to the deck.

"You tell me what to do for a change," I said to Doodad when he appeared at my side while I emptied the sink of dirty glasses, washing and stacking them to dry. "I'm good at fetching beer and doing the dishes. Not up on my mixed drinks."

"You're pretty laid-back as a boss. Most would blame me for this problem."

"Stuff happens." I shrugged. "Besides, I'm smart enough to hire good people and have sense enough to keep them."

A scream echoed off the walls, and the crowd parted slightly. It turned out that the screamer was a woman, and she was about to let another one rip when a man grabbed her arm, giving her a shake. Another man lay writhing on the floor. No one appeared too concerned. Those around him stared down into his face, not offering any assistance.

I ruled out a bar fight.

Another woman stepped up, but didn't so much as lean down in the man's direction before yelling, "We need a doctor. Man's dying."

Doodad raced out from behind the bar to investigate. Creole pointed at me and glared for me to stay put, then made his way over to the man.

"I'm a nurse." A man stepped forward. "Get my bag," he called to another man, who ran out the front door. He came back, bag in hand, in record time.

The man on the floor suddenly opened his eyes and tried to sit up, pushing away all attempts to keep him down. Bets had been placed at the bar about whether the man was living or dead, with the money running in favor of death.

Doodad pounded the bar top. "Get your boyfriend. This is a con."

I jumped up on a stepstool and yelled, "Creole."

When he turned, I motioned frantically. Doodad met him near the entrance, and after a few words, both ran out the front door. Most of the short-attention-span crowd had grown bored and were back to shouting over one another.

The maybe-dead man had turned me into a nervous wreck, and I was ecstatic to see Mac coming through the door. The only upside was that everyone had maintained their good mood and gone right back to having fun.

Mac walked behind the bar, shoving her oversized tote in a cabinet. "I would've stayed outside to help the guys, but Doodad got all bossy and told me to 'get your ass inside,'" she repeated with a dreamy smile.

I nudged her shoulder. "An update would be nice."

"You don't know?" she asked with a huge smile that got bigger when I shook my head.

"Love being the first to tell you stuff. Except maybe that I was in jail or had found another dead body—"

"Focus," I snapped.

"You had a purse-snatcher in here. Can you believe it?"

No, I couldn't, but I didn't want to stop her in the middle of her retelling.

"Dude hauled ass out the door with several bags hanging over his shoulder."

Suddenly, the "dying" man jumped to his feet without help. He darted glances over both shoulders, then beelined for the hallway and the back exit.

"Indigestion?" one man at the bar said in disbelief.

His female companion said, "More likely drunk, and the clumsy bastard tripped."

A customer banged his bottle on the bar, yelling, "How about some service down here?"

"Hold your horses, Bub," Mac yelled back. She eyed the bottle, reached into the refrigerator, and delivered the order.

"Your people skills rock." I gave her a thumbs up. "You think the guys are okay?"

"They're fine," she dismissed my concern, then set about working the bar like a pro, filling orders and keeping the banter friendly.

A woman came to the end of the bar, waving me over. "I lost my purse." To say she was sloshed would be an understatement; I had to lean in to make out her words. "Ahm…redeh ta ga… hommme naaaweh."

"Have a seat." I came around the bar and helped her onto a stool. "I believe one was turned in to the bar manager; he should be back from his break in a few minutes." It had never occurred to me that I'd need to get a sign made warning customers to beware of purse-snatchers.

The woman mumbled about her keys, feeling for pockets she didn't have. She obviously planned to drive in her current condition, but her missing purse would slow that plan and I'd keep her from getting behind the wheel. She'd either get a ride home or I'd threaten her with the police.

Pulling my phone out of my pocket, I texted Creole, "Need you inside. Woman wants her purse."

Creole texted back, "Stall."

A friend of the woman's showed up, the two enveloping each other in an effusive hug. It saved me from telling another lie about the whereabouts of her purse, which I didn't know if we had or not. Not wanting to let the woman out of my sight, I stayed close to her while I turned my attention to Mac. She treated the customers to her crazy charm, shaking the jingle bells on the front of her top every time she set a drink down. The men sat in rapt attention.

Finally, Creole and Doodad returned. Doodad had several purses slung over his shoulder, which he took to the office. When he returned, I told him about the woman and pointed her out. She and her friend had joined two men and were in the midst of a beer-bottle toast.

"Anyone inquires about a purse, they need to describe it before we hand it over," Doodad told Mac. Since there wasn't room for three behind the bar without bumping into one another, I made my exit.

I waved to the two of them, after which they immediately got caught up in conversation. I imagined Mac was getting an update. Creole leaned against the wall, wrestling with impatience.

"Heart attack guy and his friend were running a scam," he said when I got within hearing distance.

"It was rumored to be indigestion."

He laughed and hooked his arm around my shoulders. We cut through the kitchen, where I stopped and collected a to-go bag, waved to one of Cook's relatives—cousin, nephew, I couldn't remember—then headed out the exit.

"They make it a rule to hit places they don't frequent. Once inside, they scope out the exits and identify their targets. One distracts the crowd by falling on the floor; the other steals any purses that haven't been secured. Once he hits the parking lot, the other guy has a miraculous recovery and takes his leave."

Creole hit the button on his key fob, and the

locks on his truck flew up. He scooped me up, opening the door and setting me on the seat.

"How clever of you to link the two of them together."

He went around the front of the truck, climbing behind the wheel. "They weren't the brightest. The inside guy didn't pay attention to his surroundings and ran straight for the getaway car, not realizing they'd been discovered. He also didn't see the cop standing there with his accomplice already in custody. In the midst of the finger-pointing between the two men, the story came out."

"They both got arrested?" It surprised me that all that had gone unnoticed inside the bar.

"Hell, yes." He hit the steering wheel. "Or they'd be back; maybe not in Jake's, but another bar. They've pulled this scam before, and nothing short of arrest will stop their felonious activity. Even that's no assurance they won't get out and set up shop elsewhere. It wouldn't surprise me if there were a few open cases with their names on them. Right now, they're sharing a ride to jail." He gunned the engine and pulled out onto the Overseas, headed to his house.

"Kevin must not have been on duty." I squeezed my eyes shut, imagining all the ways that would have made the night worse. "He'd have closed Jake's down for the night. Even if he didn't, one sight of law enforcement and our customers would've scurried for the exits."

"You're lucky." He dropped a quick kiss on my lips at the red light. "Turns out the officer they dispatched is a friend. Assured him that the purses would get back to the rightful owners. He discussed drunk driving with Doodad, who it appears he's friends with, and was satisfied that we had that handled."

"You can bill Jake's for your protection services." I smiled at him in the dark, not sure if he could see. "The perps owe you a big thank you. If it were only me and Doodad, I'd have shot them in the butt."

Creole threw his head back and laughed.

Chapter Sixteen

'Twas the night before Christmas...

"What are you doing?" I stood in front of Creole, loosening his Santa tie, unbuttoning his shirt, and running my hands down his chest. "Much better."

"You're distracting me," he said in that deep voice that curled my toes. He winked.

"Why so fancy when even shoes are optional?"

"My girlfriend thinks I'm sexy in shorts and a tie. Bought this one special for her since she's a big Santa fan."

"She's a lucky woman."

"Salesman said it was vintage. Does that get me extra points?"

"Anything you want." I winked. I slipped into a red calypso skirt and silk scoop-neck top the saleslady had talked me into. I'd gotten a local florist to make Fab and me red wrist and ankle leis.

Creole picked up a Santa hat and smashed it down on his head, accepting my last-minute purchase with a laugh. Then he pulled me into his arms. "Are you going to behave tonight?" he growled.

"Probably not."

"Good."

I'd planned this Christmas dinner for just the four of us, and it was one of my better decisions. I wanted a drama-free, laid-back evening. Breaking with the tradition of ordering takeout, I'd whipped out an apron and spent several hours in the kitchen. That hadn't happened in years. As long as it tasted as good as it looked, the time would be worth it. Fab had special-ordered dessert and chosen the wine.

Everything had worked out perfectly, as the rest of the family had plans with their partners. We'd get together tomorrow afternoon at Mother's.

And here it was, finally happening.

The slamming of a door started us laughing.

"Some things never change. That's Fab's way of saying hurry up," I said.

Creole took my hand. "We better get down there before she comes back and starts kicking the door in."

I stopped midway down the stairs to take in the living room. All the lights, inside and out, had been turned on, and the decorations sparkled. This was my favorite time of year, and I'd especially enjoyed this one with family and friends.

Fab gestured from just inside the French doors. "Drinks are being served out here." She hadn't broken from her tradition of wearing black, having chosen a slinky, silk spaghetti-strap dress at the same store where I'd bought my dress. She'd accessorized with red stilettos that I suspected would come off after her first martini.

Earlier, Fab and I had made a seating area in front of the Christmas tree, dragging over two oversized wicker armchairs with ottomans and the copper fire pit that I'd filled with colored glass. Instead of fire, the bottom of the bowl was layered with lights.

"Where's Didier?" Creole asked.

Fab handed me a red margarita and pointed Creole to a tub of beers. "I don't know," she said with a pout.

There was a pounding on the front door. Again.

I looked at Fab. "It's not you. A little loud for you anyway."

"Burglars don't generally knock," Creole said, "so we've got that going for us. You two stay here."

"Peek through the peephole before you open the door," I said.

"Yes, ma'am."

"Ho, ho, ho," boomed from inside the house.

Fab and I had moved to the doors and peeked our heads inside. Strutting around the corner from the entry came a smoking-hot sexy Santa, booming "Ho, ho, ho" once again.

Fab squealed at her boyfriend, who was decked out in red velvet mid-thigh shorts trimmed in fur, black boots, and a hat, a big sack over his shoulder.

"Have you been a good little girl?" He leered at Fab.

"Of course not." She ran her fingers down his chest and leaned in, whispering something that had them smiling at one another.

"Santa, you've been working out." My cheeks burned.

"Way to go, dude; show me up," Creole grumbled.

Didier laughed at him and set his bag down under the stockings hanging off the end of a shelf. "You're getting coal, pal," he told Creole.

"We don't have cookies and milk for you, Santa," I said.

"This Santa wants a beer." Didier turned several bottles around, choosing one.

"And what? Drive that sleigh of yours intoxicated?" Creole asked with a laugh that Didier ignored.

"I'm happy we decided to do this," Fab said with a big smile on her face.

Dinner was over, and I was basking in the compliments.

"Since when can you cook like this?" Fab asked.

"I'm a woman of many talents," I boasted.

We moved back to sitting by the tree.

"Do you know how Fab and I met?" Didier smiled down at Fab, who stuck her tongue out.

"Good thing we've got the whole night," Creole teased.

"Let's see." I tapped my cheek. "She spied you across a crowded room and thought to herself, 'I can't live without that man.'" I swooned against Creole's chest, hand to my forehead.

"So dramatic." Fab's cheeks turned pink.

"Then…" I burst out, "you woke up tied to her bed. True love." I sighed.

Creole laughed against my neck. "Your story is missing a few details."

"Fab saved me." Didier winked at her. "It happened in the bar at the W. I was waiting for a business associate, who cancelled last-minute, and was about ready to leave when a woman sat down and proceeded to flirt hard, not willing to listen to a polite 'not interested' and go away. Next thing I know, Fab appears at the table, beautiful brown eyes snapping, telling the woman to get lost before she shoots her." He laughed.

"Which you promptly admonished me for in French." Fab smiled up at him. "The look on your face when I answered back in French was priceless."

"What happened to the woman?" I asked.

Fab shook her head as if to say, *who knows.* "Out of the blue, the bartender is announcing last call."

"I suppose it was love at first encounter," Creole said, his words tinged with sarcasm.

I crooked my head back. "Romance, babe. I love the story."

"We've been through a lot," Didier said in a low tone that conveyed how much he loved her.

Fab touched his hand. "The reality was he caught my eye. I watched him fend off that woman's blatant touchy-feely tricks and felt it was my duty to rescue the most handsome man I'd ever seen."

"I love you, Fabiana Merceau." Didier took Fab's hand, holding it in his. Fab looked up at him expectantly. "We've been through some tough times, and yet here we are, each of us always putting the other first. I can't imagine life without you."

I snuggled back against Creole's chest, and he tightened his hold.

"That's nice and mushy," Creole said in my ear.

I elbowed him lightly, not daring to laugh lest I ruin the moment.

Didier gently pushed Fab forward, standing up. He took a ring from the pocket of his Santa shorts, bending down on one knee. Focusing on her again, he whispered, "Will you marry me, love of my life?" And more words in French.

I groaned. *Damn, French again.*

Fab covered her mouth with her hands, speechless. She finally found her voice. "What if I screw everything up with my impetuousness?"

He stood and sat on the ottoman facing her. "As long as we're together, we can handle anything. We've proven that – several times.

"Yes," she said breathlessly, hugging him tightly while he put the diamond ring on her finger.

He lowered his face to hers and kissed her like she was the most desirable woman in the world. His woman. Soon to be wife.

Creole and I stood and hugged and congratulated them.

"Welcome to the family. I get a brother-in-law." I beamed at Didier.

Creole reached down and handed everyone their wine glasses.

"Merry Christmas," he toasted.

PARADISE SERIES NOVELS

Crazy in Paradise
Deception in Paradise
Trouble in Paradise
Murder in Paradise
Greed in Paradise
Revenge in Paradise
Kidnapped in Paradise
Swindled in Paradise
Executed in Paradise
Hurricane in Paradise
Lottery in Paradise
Ambushed in Paradise
Christmas in Paradise
Blownup in Paradise
Psycho in Paradise
Overdose in Paradise
Initiation in Paradise
Jealous in Paradise
Wronged in Paradise
Vanished in Paradise
Fraud in Paradise
Naive in Paradise

Deborah's books are available on Amazon
http://www.amazon.com/Deborah-Brown/e/B0059MAIKQ

About the Author

Deborah Brown is an Amazon bestselling author of the Paradise series. She lives on the Gulf of Mexico, with her ungrateful animals, where Mother Nature takes out her bad attitude in the form of hurricanes.

Remember to sign up for her newsletter to keep up-to-date with new releases and special promotions:
www.deborahbrownbooks.com

Follow on FaceBook:
facebook.com/DeborahBrownAuthor

You can contact her at Wildcurls@hotmail.com

Deborah's books are available on Amazon
amazon.com/Deborah-Brown/e/B0059MAIKQ

Made in the USA
Monee, IL
03 January 2021

56130086R00095